Silk 9

EVERYONE LIVES A STORY

Ronald Murray

© Ronald Murray

Print ISBN: 978-1-54398-108-7

eBook ISBN: 978-1-54398-109-4

This is a work of fiction. All characters, organizations, and events portrayed in this novel are products of the author's imagination or are used fictitiously.

To my wife, daughter, grand kids, family and in memory of
Della, Loman
And
Uncle George

"Magnificent Townsmen Forever"

Silk 9

EVERYONE LIVES A STORY

PART I

SILK 9
EVERYONE LIVES A STORY

CHAPTER 1

The fulgent moon cascaded down on the twenty-seven-story office building in Rosslyn, Virginia. Piercing rays of light reflected off the tinted window of the twenty-fifth-floor office suite of Reginald Saunders. "Reggie," as he was now called, stood stoically at his office window and stared out into the glistening night. He looked across the sweeping skyline and marveled as he had done so many times before at the magnificence of Washington, D.C. He stepped back to his massive mahogany desk and reached under it to push a concealed button. The mauve African silk drapes retracted and exposed the wall-length window of his office. He continued to gaze at the panoramic view across the Potomac River. To his right, he could see the Jefferson Memorial. To his left, he could see the Washington Monument and the now-lit Mall pathway leading to the Capitol. Straight across and out into the night skyline, he could see a jumbo jet in its final descent into Reagan National Airport. All the office buildings around him were now lit up as the cleaning crews were preparing to shut down the city of Rosslyn while the District was just beginning to come alive. He interrupted his gaze and turned momentarily to look around his office. To his right, he peered at the cherry wood bookshelves that stretched the entire length of the wall. The shelves had been custom built and, with a push of another button under his desk, concealed what not many people knew about: a full bathroom with a shower and another exit from his office. Also, the bookshelves housed over 100 books that he had personally read. Mostly business books from *The One Minute Manager*, to *The Company Man*, to *Black Life in Corporate America*, to *Managing in Turbulent Times* by Peter Drucker. He mused for a moment. He could teach Peter Drucker a thing or two about turbulent times. These were his private collection of business books. Having read them all was something of an accomplishment and something he was very proud of. Something they couldn't take away—not ever!

He walked around his chair and desk and across the room to the opposite wall across from his bookshelves. He took a close look at the large painting of Degas's *Dancing Women* that he had recently purchased and framed. Of course, it wasn't the original, but he had paid a hefty sum for it. Plus, the framing was almost as expensive as the painting. The painting really enhanced the feel of his office. The bright blue and green hues created a warm and relaxed environment. He made a mental note to try to refer to it as a "piece," as in a piece of art, although referring to it as a painting was quite acceptable. Now that he was gradually getting back into the art world, he wanted to be correct. As he stared at the piece of artwork, he toyed with the idea of possibly adding more art on this wall to make it look like an art gallery or museum, just like the rooms and walls filled with art when he used to visit the museums when he was a kid. This was when the white social workers would come down to his neighborhood, the hood in Northeast D.C., and round up all the kids they could find and cart them off to the museums and art galleries downtown. The social workers used to call it "cultural day." He was always fascinated by the huge European Impressionistic paintings. He later made an effort to learn all the famous painters. He would go to the library and thumb through the giant art books on Renoir, Van Gogh, Matisse, and many more.

He smiled as he reminisced about his early childhood. Being the oldest of seven children had always placed him at the forefront of everything and served as the drive and motivation to push himself. His thoughts drifted back to the question as to whether he should add more art to the wall. Maybe one day.

He turned away from the Degas and walked back across his office and across the Persian carpet that had been delivered earlier in the week. It looked great and felt plush as he stepped across it. He looked to his left and caught a glimpse of light from beneath the double oak doors of his office. That meant one thing to him: Clara, his secretary, was still working. He glanced at his Rolex watch and made a mental note to once again remind her that she shouldn't be working this late on a Friday evening. It had been a long day for them both, but now it was time to relax and enjoy the weekend and the city. But first, one more look at the skyline.

He strode back across the office to his window to take one final look. Once again, he assumed his original position with his arms crossed as he peered out into the now black night. He took a deep breath. He wanted to pinch himself as he took in the surroundings. He silently said to himself, *Reggie, it doesn't get much better than this. You've come a long way, baby, and it wasn't easy. Look at you, man. In your double-breasted Armani tailored suit; your Bally shoes; Ralph Lauren, French-cuff, custom-made shirt; diamond cufflinks from Tiffany; and Hugo Boss tie. Look at you, man. How in the hell did you make it, and who would have thought?*

CHAPTER 2

DANANG VIETNAM
TET OFFENSIVE

Technical Sgt. Eugene Johnson stood rigid in front of sixty-five shaky, frightened, and bewildered U.S. Air Force Airmen. His M-16 rifle hung loosely over his left shoulder. He adjusted his belt around his camouflage pants, pulled the bill of his fatigue cap down just above his eyes, took a deep breath, and then began to pace along the front row of young men standing in formation. He didn't speak as he sternly looked into each young man's face as he passed. No one blinked. *That's good,* he thought. *Maybe we just might get through this.*

As he neared the last man, he contemplated what he would say. He had gotten the orders earlier that morning, and it wasn't good news. *Twenty years, twenty years in the Air Force,* he thought, *and it gets down to this.*

However, he couldn't blame the Air Force because he had volunteered for duty in Vietnam. Although there were daily deaths and destruction all around, up until now there had been no immediate danger to his troops.

He slowly turned and deliberately retraced his path back toward the middle of the formation. Still, none of the eighteen, nineteen, and twenty-year-olds budged. They all knew what had happened and perhaps even why it happened, but none could visualize or think about what was going to happen. That was now Tech Sergeant Johnson's job—to turn these boys into men. As he paced, he decided he would continue to use the old basic training approach of fear and intimidation. It had worked for him during his earlier tenure as a training instructor in boot camp. Standing at six feet, three inches tall and weighing 240 pounds, he felt he could still be intimidating if need be. He was now back to the middle of the formation. He cleared his throat.

"Alright, listen up, men. To put it plain and simple, we've got a job to do. You all know the facts, except maybe Saunders and Whitehead." He eyed the two men whose names he had just called out. "These two airmen have the distinction of sleeping through a rocket attack."

Saunders and Whitehead shifted a little but managed to keep their heads and eyes straight. As sweat formed on both their brows, each knew that they were extremely lucky to be alive and standing there with the rest of the company. Airman Reginald Saunders was calling on all his faculties to remain upright. His head was still throbbing, and he felt like throwing up from all the beer he had drunk the night before—not to mention his first encounter with marijuana—compliments of his good buddy, Airman Morris Whitehead, who was standing next to him.

As if Whitehead was reading Saunders's mind, he ever so slightly turned his head toward Saunders and their eyes met briefly, just long enough to think, *We are in deep shit!*

Tech Sergeant Johnson was now standing directly in front of them. Whitehead quickly shifted his head and eyes straight ahead and, like Saunders, held his breath.

Four F-16 fighter jets flew overhead and partially drowned out all surrounding activity. A few of the airmen on the back two rows looked up into the clear sky as the jets banked and began their landing descent to the nearby base runway. Tech Sergeant Johnson looked up briefly, revealing just a bit of his honey-brown face and piercing dark eyes. He waited for the sound of the jets to diminish before he rested his gaze back on Saunders and Whitehead.

He bellowed out his next words, and Saunders and Whitehead could feel the heat from his breath. "Alpha Barracks was hit by two enemy rockets last night. Three airmen were killed and sixteen seriously wounded. We at Beta Barracks were lucky. As most of us now know, we only sustained three minor injuries and light damage to the barracks from shrapnel. So what do we do now?"

Tech Sergeant Johnson knew he would get no response from the young men. He gestured over his shoulder.

"Those F-16s you just saw coming in and those booming noises," he pointed directly behind him in the direction of the visible but distant mountain range, "they are for real, gentlemen. We hit 'Charlie' hard last night. For those of you who haven't figured it out yet, 'Charlie' is the Viet Cong, the enemy. And we haven't finished yet. It's going to get a lot louder around here, so get used to it. You may be wondering why you were issued M-16 rifles earlier this morning. As I said, it's quite simple. We've got a job to do. I know it's been a while since you went through basic training, and most of you thought it was fun and games.

You thought you would never see a rifle again. After all, you are in the Air Force, right? You are supposed to fly and to support flying, right?"

There was some shifting by the young men, but no response to the sergeant's question.

"Wrong, gentlemen. You have been, and as you all know by now, in Danang, Vietnam in the demilitarized zone where there is still a war going on, and gentlemen, war is hell!

"You had better get reacquainted with your rifle, because in a few days, or even hours, it may be the best friend you have and your only source of survival. I received orders this morning that 'Charlie' broke the outer perimeter of the base on the north side and made it through the Marines. We took a lot of casualties. Reinforcements are on the way. In the meantime, someone has to hold down the fort."

Tech Sergeant Johnson paused and looked Saunders and Whitehead directly in the eyes. "Guess who?"

Whitehead shifted his weight. Saunders felt nauseous. The men as a group stirred. Tech Sergeant Johnson could sense the apprehension and perhaps a little fear in the men. He stepped back.

"So here we are, gentleman. You've been issued your rifles and your K-rations. Unfortunately, we aren't going to have room service for the next few days."

The sergeant could see a few smiles as the group stirred.

"You've got your bayonets, which if needed, can be attached to your rifles and your helmets, which you had better get used to wearing. You have water canteens, ammo belts, and enough extra ammunition to fight two wars."

He took a brief second and looked through the ranks. He observed that a lot of the young men, including Saunders and Whitehead, were wearing ammunition belts crisscrossed like an X across their bodies. He wanted to scream but thought better of it.

He continued. "Now Lieutenant Colonel Rollins, you remember him, don't you? He's the one who threw the big party."

He glanced at Saunders and Whitehead.

"Apparently, some of us never left the party, now did we? Lieutenant Colonel Rollins is also the man we work for, and he'll be joining us shortly. Anyway, he asked me whether or not we were ready."

He stepped closer to Saunders and Whitehead. He shouted over their heads to all the men, "You know what I told him?"

All Saunders and Whitehead could see was the cold darkness of the Sergeant's eyes and his pearly white teeth. Saunders wasn't sure, but as he heard the rhetorical question, he thought he saw foam in the corner of the sergeant's mouth. Tech Sergeant Johnson paused for effect. He knew this was the moment. Either he was going to make them or break them. He stepped back, sucked in his stomach and shouted. Spit flew into Saunders and Whitehead's faces.

"I told him, 'You damned right, sir.' I told him that there's no way 'Charlie' is going to break the inner perimeter of this base and get to the planes on the runways. There's no way 'Charlie' will see an F-16 fighter or helicopter unless it's from the sky raining down a hail of bullets on his ass!" He yelled even louder. "I told Lieutenant Colonel Rollins that we"—he paused and shook his fist—"Beta Company would blow 'Charlie's' ass back to kingdom come. We may not be the Marines, but we can fight—and there's a debt to be repaid. We knew those three airmen who were killed last night. So was I right, Saunders? Was I right, Whitehead?"

Both Saunders and Whitehead jumped and somehow managed to say in unison, "Yes, sir!"

Tech Sergeant Johnson leaned his face between the two young men. Saunders could feel his knees knocking. Perspiration on the sergeant's face was now visible and dripped from his forehead.

"I can't hear you!"

Saunders and Whitehead repeated their response even louder. "Yes, sir!"

Tech Sergeant Johnson leaned forward and walked briskly down the formation of men. "Was I right?"

Beta Company shouted back, "Yes, sir!"

He shouted, "I can't hear you!"

"Yes, sir!"

"I can't hear you!"

"Yes, sir!"

"All right then. You know your positions and assignments. The only Viet Cong I want to see through that perimeter fence," he pointed behind him about 200 yards out, "is a dead bastard! Let's kick some ass! Move out!"

The men let out another earth-shattering roar and quickly broke ranks.

Tech Sergeant Johnson watched as they quickly dispersed and assumed their positions. He said to himself,

Boys being asked to do what men should be doing.

His thoughts were interrupted as he looked over his shoulder and saw Lieutenant Colonel Walter Rollins stepping out of his jeep and approaching him. Rollins was in his mid-forties, so he was a little older than the thirty-eight-year-old Johnson. He was of medium height and build, slightly graying around the temples, and rather unassuming as far as Johnson was concerned. However, he was a seasoned veteran, a career man, and was now doing his second tour of Vietnam. Rollins had pretty much allowed Johnson to handle the company as he saw fit.

Johnson remembered the first day he reported to duty. Rollins simply told him, "You watch my back, and we are going to get along fine."

Johnson respected the man for that because even though the Air Force was integrated and there was a war going on, it still wasn't often that a white officer would step aside and actually allow his subordinate, a black man, to run things. Tech Sergeant Johnson snapped to attention and saluted. Lieutenant Colonel Rollins returned the salute.

"At ease, sergeant."

Johnson relaxed. Rollins continued, "I overheard a little of your address to Beta."

"Yes, sir."

"What do you think?"

"Well sir, if I could be frank—"

"Please, sergeant, be candid."

"Well, sir, these are boys. They are untrained, untested, and emotionally unequipped to be in this war. Most don't know why they are here. They are a long way from home, and they are scared as shit. Frankly, I don't think we have a rat's chance in hell if 'Charlie' gets through the Marines and breaks the inner perimeter."

Rollins was surprised by Johnson's response. He cleared his throat. "Well, I guess we had better keep our fingers crossed."

Johnson looked at Rollins and said, "I'm doing one better, sir."

"What?"

"I'm saying a little prayer."

Lieutenant Colonel Rollins cleared his throat again, and as he walked away from Johnson, softly said, "Well, carry on, sergeant, and good luck."

Tech Sergeant Johnson stepped back, saluted, and in a toned-down voice replied, "Yes sir, colonel."

CHAPTER 3

Airmen Reginald Saunders and Airman Morris Whitehead sat with their backs against the dirt wall of the foxhole they had dug the day before. Two days had passed since Tech Sergeant Johnson addressed the young men of Beta Company. Saunders and Whitehead had the distinct pleasure of sharing their position at the specific request of Tech Sergeant Johnson. It had been a long day for them and the rest of the troops that formed a two-hundred-yard column of two men fox holes spaced exactly thirty feet apart. Their fully loaded M-16 rifles sat on tripods atop sandbags. No one had detected any Viet Cong yet, but the sounds of war were all around the men; fighter jets, bombers, and Huey helicopter gunships were constantly flying overhead, and bombs were detonating well within earshot. Occasional flashes of light and tracers rocketed across the sky, all indicators that the situation had heated up. The company had been briefed earlier by Tech Sergeant Johnson, who informed them that nothing had changed and to remain on full alert. Whitehead looked at his rifle and turned to Saunders.

"You think we are ever going to use those?"

"I don't know, man. All I know is I'm sick and tired of eating K-rations and swatting these damn flies. Plus, this damn heat is getting to me. I haven't had a shower in . . . I can't remember when!"

Whitehead laughed. "Hey, you think you are at the Ritz Hotel or something? It could be monsoon season. With all the rain and flooding, we would probably be swimming in these foxholes. Man, it could be worse."

Saunders looked at Whitehead. "How could it be worse, man? You know we only have two months before we ship out of this hellhole. Two months and we're back to the States. Man, I don't need to be dealing with this."

Whitehead detected Saunders was getting a little excited as he often did, so Whitehead thought his best bet would be to try to calm Saunders down. "Look, man, you don't have anything to worry about. We are going to make it back." He added, "Hey, if our time was up, we would have been in Alpha Barracks when those rockets hit. Just take it easy."

Saunders popped open a can of K-rations and picked out a chocolate chip cookie. He rolled his eyes as he placed it in his mouth. Whitehead noticed and thought to himself that for a guy who was constantly complaining about the canned food, Saunders was doing a pretty good job of devouring the contents in them. He continued talking. "You see, man, all you have to do is think positive things like we did yesterday. You know, you tell me a little more about yourself, and I tell you a little more about me. Hey, before long, time will fly by, and all this will be over. Besides, ain't no way 'Charlie' is going to get through the Marines. So relax, my man ... Relax."

Saunders popped another cookie and remained silent. Whitehead felt he had to keep probing, if for no other reason than to hear himself talk. Nightfall was beginning to set in. More bombs and explosions could be heard off in the distance. Sporadic splashes and arching red light from tracers could be seen racing across the sky, then disappearing behind the tops of trees. Whitehead sure as hell hoped their aircraft and Marines were hitting their targets.

"Now let me see if I've got this right, Saunders. I know you have mentioned this to me before, but since we are here sitting in the dark, let's go over it one more time. You were born and raised in Washington, D.C., right? You've got three, four, no, six brothers and sisters. Man, that's a big family. And you are the oldest, right? And back home everyone calls you Reggie. Now, let's see, you lived in the hood but managed to get through high school. You played baseball—Mr. Hotshot, according to you. After high school, you joined the Air Force because you feared the draft would catch up with you, and you wanted no part of Vietnam, but here you are. . . Go figure. So, have I got it right?"

Saunders nonchalantly nodded.

Whitehead had a devious look on his face. "See. There you go, Saunders. You know that's not all of it."

"What?"

"You know what . . . or should I say who? Come on, man, you are holding back on me. Tell me about your girl." He nudged Saunders, who showed a little life and smiled.

"Naw, man I'm not getting into that."

"Come on, Saunders. It's you and me, good buddy. Suppose you don't make it back. Somebody's got to tell her, right?" Whitehead pointed to himself.

Saunders laughed and elbowed him in the ribs. "Man, you are sick. I don't know how I let you talk me into this stuff. Come to think about it, that's the reason why we are in deep you-know-what with Tech Sergeant Johnson." Saunders began to speak in a high whining voice. "One more drink, Saunders, one more drink. Then try a puff of this, Saunders. The next thing I know is that I'm three sheets to the wind, messed up, passed out, and sleeping through a rocket attack!"

Whitehead interjected, "Hey, but now that you are still here—was it fun or what?"

Saunders looked over at Whitehead, stared for a moment, then broke out in laughter, slapping Whitehead's hand. Another bomb explosion was heard off into the distance. The ground around them shook and interrupted their conversation. There were several minutes of silence before Saunders said, "Tracey."

"What?"

"Her name is Tracey."

Whitehead perked up, "Yeah, okay, go on."

"Man, I've told you all this before."

"Yeah, but never about your girl. I want to make sure I get it right, just in case you don't make it back."

Although Whitehead was joking, Saunders had a serious look on his face and was thinking to himself, *What if I don't make it back?* So he continued.

"Well, she's just everything to me. The reason why I breathe, I guess. We started dating in high school, our junior year. You know, did the usual stuff. In our senior year, we went to the prom. We stayed out all night. Went to a beach party and made love on the beach. Man, I'll never forget that night. She was so fine."

Saunders paused as if he were daydreaming. "Anyway, we stayed out until noon the next day. Her parents were pissed as hell, but hey, it was a night that I would do all over again if I had the chance."

Whitehead interrupted again. "So what's the deal now, man?"

"Well, her parents wanted her to go to college. Her old man is a doctor, and her mom is Mrs. Socialite. So you can imagine how they felt about me being from the hood and all. Anyway, they definitely wanted to get her off to school and out of D.C. So she went down south to college, and I joined the Air Force. I started writing to her at home as soon as I arrived in Vietnam." Saunders stopped mid-sentence. Silence drifted in, and his face changed. He hesitated before continuing. "But I haven't heard from her."

Whitehead stirred a little and was thinking to himself, *Man, that sounds messed up.* But he only said, "So it's been almost a year that you haven't heard from her?'

Saunders didn't respond right away. He just stared, seemingly thinking to himself. Then he said softly, "Yeah, but, I guess she's busy with school and all, you know."

Whitehead thought about responding but decided against it. He just nodded.

Saunders then added, "Anyway, in two months, I'll be back. I'll catch up with her, and hey, we'll take it from there."

There was a moment when neither man said anything. Saunders realized that he needed to change the subject, so he quickly said, "So, Whitehead, what's your story? Like how in the heck did you get here to screw my life up?"

Whitehead sat up straight and said, "Well, man, like I told you. I have one brother and one sister—about half the size of your family. I'm the youngest. I was born and raised in Chicago, and back home, they call me Morris. Both my parents were teachers, so we led a decent lifestyle. Not rich or anything, just okay, you know. Anyway, I never liked school. Thought it was a big waste of my time. I did play a little baseball, though, and a little tennis. I finished high school—didn't want to go to college, which really pissed my parents off. I did little odd jobs. Like you, I wanted no part of the draft, figured I didn't want to go in the Army and wind up in Vietnam. Thought about Canada, but chickened out. So I joined the Air Force. Damned bright decision, wasn't it?"

Saunders laughed and passed over a cookie from his K-rations. Whitehead took one.

"Hey, and that's about it."

"What about a girlfriend?"

"Naw, not me, man. I played the field the entire time I was in school. Too many women to just settle on one. Talking about prom night. Man, I had two women. Of course, they didn't know about each other."

Saunders perked up in disbelief. "No way, man!"

"Hey, if I'm lying, I'm flying. It was tight, but I pulled it off and got a double banger that night."

Saunders rolled his eyes and said, "Get out of here!"

Neither spoke for a moment. They just sat there listening to the sounds of bombs and sporadic small-arms fire.

Saunders broke the silence between the two men. "You know, Whitehead, I didn't like you when we first met on K.P. duty. You were so arrogant."

"Yeah, I know for some reason that's the first impression people get with me. But then came the baseball game, and now we are legends in our own time."

Saunders shook his head. "Well, I wouldn't go so far as to say that, but I was happier than hell when Lieutenant Colonel Rollins came into the mess hall that night and inquired about a rumor he heard that I played baseball in high school and was a pitcher. And then you raised your potato-spud hand saying that you were an infielder."

Whitehead chimed in, "Yeah, who would have imagined that old Lieutenant Colonel Rollins was a baseball freak?"

Saunders added, "Of course, the whole thing was for bragging rights and being top dog on the base."

Whitehead began to reminisce. "Yeah, man, that was one heck of a baseball game. At the time, Saunders, I would have bet a hundred bucks that you wouldn't have been able to pitch your way out of a wet paper bag. And there we were in the top of the ninth inning with us in the lead, one to zip. You had a two-hit shutout going. What happened after that, homeboy, was the stuff of legends. We'll be telling our grandkids one day."

"Yeah, now that I think about it, it was pretty remarkable, huh?"

"Remarkable? Hey man, you struck out the sides. Delta Company never knew what hit them. You were so smooth, man, so smooth. That's why I called you Silk. Now everybody is calling you that."

Saunders smiled at the thought of being somewhat of a celebrity on base with the lower ranks of men.

"Hey, it's like I told you at the bar the other night. You know, before I got wasted. I wouldn't have been in that spot to preserve the win if you hadn't been Mr. Vacuum Cleaner at shortstop. What did you make? Three or four game-saving stops? I mean, nothing got through you all day. And what about that diving save in the hole behind second base in the bottom of the eighth? You hit the ground, got up, and fired the guy out at first. Man, you had some heat on that ball. And I guess we just have to mention your double in the seventh that drove in our only run."

Whitehead smiled. "Yeah, that was awesome, wasn't it? One heck of a game. Not to mention our reward for being the Co-MVPs and making Lieutenant Colonel Rollins the 'Man' on base for a while."

Saunders added, "Yeah, one week of R&R in Hong Kong. Talking about an experience. I thought I had died and gone to heaven. Remember when we went to that bar, you know, the one they called Motown USA?"

Whitehead answered, "Oh yeah, the music was blasting Smokey and the Temps. And there were wall-to-wall women and mostly brothers in the place. We looked down the bar at all those beautiful Asian women with long straight black hair, smooth olive complexion, and almond eyes. All we had to do was pick one out, pay the 'Mama-san' five bucks, and they were ours for the entire night. They spoke perfect English and loved the brothers, man. They took us all around the city and showed us where to buy those sharkskin suits, cameras, and those gigantic stereo speakers that we shipped back home. Cheap man, real cheap."

Saunders asked, "You remember the names of the two we wound up with?"

"Which two? Hell, we must have gone back to that bar four times to exchange women. Shit, man, I can't remember."

"I mean the last two. The ones we kept for more than one day."

"Naw, I can't remember, but I did write their names on the back of the pictures we took. Got to show them to all the homeboys when I get back. Yeah man, they were fine and definitely knew how to make you forget about the war. What a week . . . What a week."

They both slapped hands before sitting in silence and listened to the steady sounds of bombardment in the distance.

CHAPTER 4

Fifty yards down the line, Airman John Watson and Airman Frank Davis sat in their foxhole wondering whether they would ever make it back to the States. As Air Force support personnel, they too were nervous about their new responsibility and predicament. It was definitely not what they had signed up for. Airman Davis, who was white, had just finished telling Airman Watson, who was black, about his early childhood growing up on the family farm in Georgia. Watson was about to share his early childhood growing up in New York when Davis put his hand up and said, "You see that?"

Watson leaned forward and took position at his M-16 rifle. "See what?"

Davis had already assumed a firing position. "See that out there! There's movement. They're coming, man. They're coming!"

Before Watson could respond, Davis opened up firing rapid burst into the darkness. Watson said, "Aw shit!" and supported his partner with a volley of rounds. The men to the right and left started firing, and there were clouds of smoke, dust, and sparks about one hundred yards out.

The sudden, deafening sounds of rifles firing all around them startled Saunders and Whitehead.

Whitehead said, "What the . . ."

They lunged at their weapons, released the safety catches, put on their helmets, and tightened their straps. They both opened fire. Whitehead shot in controlled single bursts. Saunders flipped his rifle to automatic and squeezed the trigger. His shoulder vibrated as if he was operating a jackhammer. It stung like hell, but he continued to squeeze as hundreds of bullets spewed from his rifle. He could feel the heat and see the smoke and sparks of light as the bullets ricocheted off the perimeter fence. The noise was deafening, but he kept his finger squeezing the trigger and his hand holding his rifle steady. Dirt was now in his eyes and partially blinding him. It seemed like an eternity, but he could hear a faint voice somewhere. However, his finger was still glued on the trigger, and he continued to fire. Then there was a sudden jerk on his shoulder that momentarily disengaged him from his rifle.

"Silk! It's over, man. It's over!"

It was Whitehead holding Saunders's right hand down and away from his rifle. "Tech Sergeant Johnson gave the command to cease fire a minute ago!"

Sweat was pouring from Saunders dirt-filled face. His eyes appeared to be in a trance as if he were a deer in front of headlights. He was trembling, shaking, and breathing hard—almost hyperventilating.

Whitehead yelled, "Are you alright? I called you at least three times before I decided to just shove you. You were in some kind of zone, man."

Saunders sat back against the dirt wall, still shaking. "Did we get them?"

"I don't know, man, but from what I can see, there is going to be one heck of a troop detail repairing the perimeter fence. We shot the hell out of it."

As the sounds of the distant bombs and small arms fire faded into the night like thunder rolling through a valley, there seemed to be a relative calm for the first time in days. Saunders and Whitehead could hear Tech Sergeant Johnson's voice coming down the ranks. They heard the command, "Beta Company—fall in!"

Both Whitehead and Saunders jumped from their foxhole and followed the rest of the company to formation.

After they were assembled, Tech Sergeant Johnson addressed them, "It's over, men. . . . It's over. I just got the orders. I don't know who started the firing down the line. I didn't give the command, but I guess it's good to know that you all responded." He asked the question: "Did we get 'Charlie?'" He paused. "No, because 'Charlie' didn't get through the Marines."

There were a lot of puzzled looks peering back at the sergeant.

He continued, "However, what we did get was enough beef to have one hell of a barbecue. It appears we killed ten cows, men. Ten very dead cows. Somehow they got away from a local peasant and got between the outer and inner perimeter fences of the base."

Tech Sergeant Johnson's face became sterner as he looked down the ranks. He was thinking about all the ridiculing and joking he was going to get from his peers, and perhaps he should just let it all hang out with his men. Really rip them. Let them experience some of the heat. Although it was funnier than hell, he was glad that no one got hurt in the hail of gunfire. These were boys a few days ago, and he thought that now they'd become men. He looked in the direction of Saunders and Whitehead.

"The good news from my vantage point, men, is that you responded. And you responded with fierceness and guts. I'm real proud of you, and I know without a doubt that had there been Viet Cong coming through that fence, they would have been some dead sons of bitches!"

The men let out a thunderous roar, and Tech Sergeant Johnson smiled for maybe the first time since he had been in Vietnam.

"Good job, men. Gather your gear and return to the barracks. Report for regular duty at 06:00 tomorrow. We'll let the Marines do what they do best. We'll repair the fence, collect some beef, and get back to flying some aircraft. Shower up, and get some sleep. Fall out."

CHAPTER 5

Tech Sergeant Johnson rustled the stack of paperwork on his desk. He had been putting off the inevitable for days. Now it was crunch time, and he knew he had to begin processing and distributing Beta Company's exit orders from Vietnam. His men would be well happy, he knew. Half the company would be leaving in a few days and the other half within the following ten days. He began to sort the file names alphabetically as he silently read the destinations of each. He came to Airmen Reginald Saunders file, opened it, read the destination, and shook his head. "Not bad."

He also looked at his watch, which indicated 06:55. "That kid had better be on time or I'll . . . "

Just then, Airman Saunders walked into the Sergeant's office, which was on the second level of a converted barrack. Johnson rose from his desk.

"Glad you could make it, airman."

"You wanted to see me, Tech Sergeant?"

"No, not me, son—Lieutenant Colonel Rollins. Follow me."

Saunders followed Tech Sergeant Johnson out of his office and down the hallway to Lieutenant Colonel Rollins's office. Johnson knocked lightly.

"Come in, sergeant."

Johnson poked his head in the doorway and said, "Sir, I have Airman Saunders."

"Good, sergeant. Show him in—and that will be all."

Tech Sergeant Johnson opened the door stepped aside and allowed Saunders to enter. He then went over to Rollins and handed him Saunders's file. Saunders was still somewhat puzzled, but he instinctively saluted the colonel who was now rising from his desk. The colonel returned the salute.

"Sit down, Saunders."

Saunders relaxed and sat down in one of the two chairs directly in front of the colonel's desk. Tech Sergeant Johnson quietly shut the door behind him.

Lieutenant Colonel Rollins thumbed through Saunders's file and didn't speak for a moment. Saunders took the opportunity to look around what he had determined to be a fairly stark office. Nothing really spectacular. Just the standard gray metal military desk, a small bookcase with military manuals over in one corner, a steel gray file cabinet, and an American flag. There was a small window directly behind the colonel that Saunders could see the next barracks over. It opened the small room up a little. Beyond that, the office appeared typically military—no frills. Lieutenant Colonel Rollins looked up from the file.

"I guess you are wondering why I asked to see you?"

Saunders uncrossed his legs and straightened in the chair. "Uh, I'm not sure, sir."

"Relax, Saunders. This should be all good. I wanted to make sure your orders were processed as I had instructed."

Saunders looked confused. He couldn't figure out where the colonel was going, but experience had taught him in these types of situations to just remain calm and do what he always did. He held his breath.

"You see, Saunders, I wanted to make good on that promise I made to you. You play on the ball team; we win. I pull a few strings, call in a couple of notes, and we get you out of here." Rollins glanced down at the file and said, "Everything looks in place, and by the way, thanks again for pitching one hell of a ball game."

Saunders exhaled and nodded. "Thank you, sir."

The colonel continued, "You know, Saunders, I have to be frank with you. My back was against the wall with that damn baseball game. I had been the brunt of all the jokes imaginable around this place. Beta Company had never won, and I was growing wary of the possibility of getting our butts kicked again. So when Tech Sergeant Johnson came to me and said you could pitch, I was somewhat skeptical. However, the sergeant has a gift for evaluating men. So he persuaded me, and hell, the rest is history. Where'd you learn to pitch like that, son?"

Saunders was somewhat surprised by the colonel's comments but managed to respond. "Well, sir, it just all started when I was a kid in our neighborhood. We played stickball in the streets a lot. And for some reason, I always got picked to throw the tennis ball. I guess I got good at it along the way. The social workers used to bus us across town to a new recreation center, and I started playing Little League baseball. Then one day, I decided to try out for my high school team. Won a few games and pitched a six-hitter in the city championship game. I tried out for the Washington Senators professional baseball team and made it up to the final cut. They said I was good but a little too small for the majors. I needed to bulk up. Never got around to lifting weights, but I got a couple of baseball scholarships for college and was about to check into them when my father had a heart attack and lost his construction job. About the same time, my mother was laid off her job of cleaning office buildings. Being the oldest of seven children and already on welfare and all—well, I had to help the family. So baseball and school were put on hold. I was afraid of the draft and decided to join up." Saunders hunched his shoulders. "So here I am."

Rollins sat back in his chair and shook his head. "Hell of a story, Saunders, and you are one hell of a baseball player. I'm still collecting on all my bets, and I'm happier than a dog with two dicks. So all that's left is where you are going?"

Saunders perked up because up until this moment he had no idea. He knew the military could send him anywhere and that he had no chance of getting back to D.C., but he definitely didn't want to go anywhere cold.

So come on, colonel, lay it on me, man—Florida would be great, he thought.

"How does California grab you?"

"California, uh, hadn't thought much about . . ."

"Land of sunshine and fun. I'm talking San Francisco."

Saunders's eyes lit up. "San Francisco, uh, that sounds great, sir."

"Well, it's a done deal. I've already sent a letter off introducing you to whom you will be reporting. His name is Major Nathan Maxwell, a good friend of mine. I told him all about you." Lieutenant Colonel Rollins leaned forward and had a serious look on his face. "Now there's one final thing, Saunders."

Saunders straightened up again.

"I don't usually get too involved with the men who report to me. But you did me one hell of a favor and got me out of a jam—saved my butt. Looking through your file, it's evident that you are an intelligent young man. One could even argue that you probably didn't belong here. You scored very high on your military entrance exam. You've aced every military manual exam. You've attained the rank of sergeant, and you've only been in the service for eighteen months. Hell, if there weren't a war going on, you could have easily qualified for Officer's Candidate School. You've got that raw and rare talent of a leader."

Lieutenant Colonel Rollins paused and leaned across his desk. Saunders shifted in the now-uncomfortable chair.

Rollins continued, "So, I've gone out on a limb. You are to report to Major Maxwell, and you will be his personal assistant. So duty should be fairly light for the remainder of your four-year hitch. With all the free time you should have, I strongly suggest that you get back to school. You know, use the G. I. Bill and start taking some college courses. Use that head of yours for something besides getting it clogged up with dope and alcohol."

Saunders attempted to explain, "Well, sir, I . . . "

Rollins cut him off. "No explanation needed. You're young, and we all make mistakes. The trick is to learn from your mistakes. So there you have it, airman. I can lead you to water, but I can't make you drink."

Rollins shut Saunders's file, rose from his desk, and said, "Good luck, airman, and dismiss."

Saunders rose and saluted. "Thank you, sir."

As Saunders exited the Lieutenant Colonel's office and walked down the hallway, a great deal happier than he had been on the original trip, he stopped by Tech Sergeant Johnson's office. He wanted to personally thank him and say goodbye. He knocked on the open door and was about to enter as Tech Sergeant Johnson looked up from his desk.

"Uh, Tech Sergeant, I just wanted to say . . . "

Before he could finish, Tech Sergeant Johnson raised his hand and said, "No need to thank me, son. I'm just glad you made it. Don't get into any trouble when you get back to the States. I hear California is a happening place."

Saunders smiled.

"Good luck, son."

"Thanks, Tech Sergeant."

Tech Sergeant Johnson returned to sorting through the papers on his desk. Saunders took the hint and continued down the hallway.

The telephone rang, and Johnson picked up the receiver. It was Lieutenant Colonel Rollins. "Well, what do you think, sergeant?"

"It's like I told you earlier, sir. I think he's an intelligent kid, but with his background, who knows? I appreciate you going out on a limb in getting him with Major Maxwell. I hope it won't be egg on your face."

Rollins laughed. "Well, it won't be the first time, sergeant. Hey, and by the way, thanks for a job well done. I know you are getting out of here soon."

"Thank you, sir. All in a year's work. It'll be great getting back to the States, and thanks for getting me back to Mississippi. My family loves the fact that I'll be close to home now."

"Well, you earned it, sergeant. I'll talk to you before you get out of here."

Johnson put the receiver down, leaned back in his chair, and smiled. He thought, *A few more weeks and I'm getting the hell out of Vietnam.*

CHAPTER 6

The C-130 cargo jet roared its engines as it sat on the runway. The four camouflaged refueling trucks had just pulled away from feeding it thousands of gallons of jet fuel in preparation for the twenty-three-hour flight back to the United States. The great silver bird looked like a five-story apartment building. It was the workhorse for troop movement to and from Vietnam.

Three companies, including Airmen from Beta Company, casually stood in their fatigues about seventy-five feet from the behemoth. Fifty or so of them made up a small but happy contingent of several armed forces units preparing to leave Vietnam. All their worldly personal items were stuffed in enormous duffel bags. Most of the men had already shipped the heavier collectibles, such as stereos, tape players, CB radios, and clothing—like sharkskin suits, custom-made silk shirts, and gabardine slacks—a month or so earlier. It was a festive mood as the men took photos together, shook hands, and hugged each other.

Airman Reginald Saunders and Airman Morris Whitehead slapped hands and hugged. Saunders stepped back from Whitehead and said, "Hey, we made it."

"Yeah, I know, man, but I have to admit, I'm going to miss you, Silk."

"Hey, it won't be too bad. Besides, it's a long flight back."

They both smiled.

"Hey, but like I said, we'll stay in touch."

Whitehead nodded his head and said, "Yeah, so we'll stay in touch, right?"

"Right."

They both looked at each other for a moment before Whitehead spoke. "I know we can talk on the plane back, but we are probably going to be sleeping most of the way, so what's your game plan when you get back, man?"

Saunders grinned. "Well, you know I got my thirty-days leave coming before I report out in California. So, I'm heading back to D.C. to see my family and all. Then I'm renting a car . . . "

Whitehead interrupted, "I thought you were buying a car as soon as you got back?"

"Yeah, I thought about it, but I'm not thrilled with the idea of driving cross country to California. So, I'm going to wait until I get out there and then look around for some reliable transportation. Anyway, I'm going to rent a car and drive down to see Tracey."

Whitehead stepped back a little and said, "Oh, I didn't know you had heard from her."

Saunders knew that Whitehead was not going to let the matter drop so he decided to 'fess up. "Well, I haven't really heard from her. I wrote to her and just told her when I'd be there."

"So you are just going to show up?"

"Well, yeah, what's wrong with that? I wrote to her and told her I was coming."

"Yeah, but she didn't write back."

"Hey, cool it, man. It'll be okay. I can handle it. I've got it all figured out."

"Yeah, well, I sure hope so, man."

Saunders was about to add to his explanation when Tech Sergeant Johnson's voice boomed over the roar of the C-130's engines.

"Alright, you lucky stiffs—time to move it out. We still got a war going on over here, and some of us have to still clean up the mess. So get moving." The sergeant relaxed and added, "And by the way, men—thanks for a job well done. Have a safe trip home, and good luck."

Saunders, along with troops from Beta Company, picked up their duffel bags, said a few last goodbyes, and filed past the sergeant while each shook his hand.

Saunders shook Whitehead's hand. "We made it, man; we actually made it. If I don't get a chance to say it again before we hit the States, I'll keep in touch, Morris."

"You bet, Silk."

As they lined up to board the plane, Saunders looked up from the tarmac at the now-blue skies. In another world, it would be a pretty sight, but the distant sound of bombs exploding reminded him that Vietnam was still a hellhole.

The massive rear door of the C-130 opened. Saunders paused and took one last look at the distant wasteland around him. A single file of new troops was coming down the ramp and departing the plane. An air of silence prevailed as both lines of troops looked at each other. Some were older, but many were younger than Saunders. It now hit him that he was one of the lucky ones. He was going home. They, like him, would have to endure thirteen months or more in this foreign hellhole they called Vietnam. He looked at each solemn face as they passed, thinking to himself, *Some will be lucky and make it back, and some will not.*

CHAPTER 7

BACK IN THE STATES

Spring usually was a great time to be on a college campus, especially just before mid-terms, because of the anticipation of leaving to return home for spring break. The campus in Hampton Roads, Virginia was no exception. It sparkled with patches of green grass interwoven with historic walkways leading to the various campus buildings. Students, attempting to study, were sprawled on blankets, some in just their jeans and T-shirts, on the grassy areas. However, most just soaked up the brilliant rays of sunlight and the sudden warmth of the spring air.

Tracey Marshall looked down from her second-floor sorority house window. Her room was directly over the insignia bolted to the stone building. When passersby looked up at the insignia, they could always determine whether she or her sorority sister was in. She briefly watched her fellow students scurrying about the campus on their way to classes, the library, the cafeteria, or whatever. She walked back to her desk and the three thick psychology books that were opened. She glanced at her watch and noted that her allotted time for studying was over. She had to get ready for her lunch date. She sat on her bed and contemplated what she would wear when the phone rang. She picked up and heard Renee, one of her sorority sisters.

"Tracey?"

"Yes."

"You have a visitor here to see you."

Renee elongated the word "visitor," which Tracey knew meant a male was in the house. She looked at her watch again in puzzlement. She had been expecting Clayton, but he had indicated a much later time.

Oh, well, he must be early, she thought.

"Tell him I'll be right down."

She hung up the receiver, sprung from the bed, grabbed her makeup bag, and dashed out of her room and down the hallway to the bathroom. As she looked at herself in the mirror, she realized that she had a lot of work to do that would require more time. She smiled and said to herself, *He'll just have to wait. Serves him right for being early.*

CHAPTER 8

The map didn't make any sense to Reggie. He sat in the parking lot of the rental company in the rented Chevrolet and turned the map upside down. *Nope, that doesn't work either. Military maps are much easier,* he thought. There was a point A and a point B. You just drew the line between the two, and you reached your destination. Had the rental attendant given him the wrong map? He flipped the unfolded map over and rechecked the outside heading. It read: "Map of Virginia."

Damn, he thought. *How hard can it be to find Hampton Roads, Virginia?*

He knew it was south of Richmond. In disgust, he threw the map on the backseat of the Chevy, punched the car in drive, and headed out of the parking lot. He said to himself, *I'm just going to find Interstate 95 South and keep going until I hit Richmond. Then if I don't see signs, I'll stop and ask somebody for directions.*

He had been driving close to two hours when he saw the signs that indicated Hampton Roads—follow Rt. 64 East. He relaxed now that he knew he was on his way. The drive had been rather smooth and relatively uneventful, except for the fact that his favorite D.C. soul radio station had faded out. In actuality, he was only half-listening most of the time because he was thinking about what he was going to say to Tracey. Although he had been home for a couple of days visiting with his family and had sufficient time to figure out what to say, he hadn't come up with anything that made him feel comfortable. He had rehearsed questions and explanations, but nothing seemed to fit. Finally, he had given up and admitted that all he wanted was for things to go back to where they were before he left for the Air Force and Vietnam. No questions, no explanations . . . just back to the ways things used to be. Two people madly in love with one another.

What could be simpler than that? he thought.

He put on his blinker and turned onto the Rt. 64 East exit ramp.

Approximately forty-five minutes later, he arrived in Hampton Roads and followed the signs for the college. Fifteen minutes later, he was on the campus and stopped at the security building for directions to the living quarters of a Ms. Tracey Marshall.

CHAPTER 9

Tracey Marshall took one final glance in the mirror and smiled.

Time to knock his socks off, she thought.

She picked up her toiletries off the counter, rushed out of the bathroom, threw them in her room, and raced down the hallway and down the stairs to the reception area.

Reggie had been indulging in a current issue of *Jet* magazine when he heard footsteps and looked up. He almost choked, and his eyes became glassy when he saw her. She was the most beautiful woman he had ever seen. She was like a Greek goddess with her slender body, silky smooth skin, and glossy hair that was much longer than Reggie had remembered. Tracey slowed her pace down the stairs when she realized it was Reggie.

"Oh my God. Reggie, what in the world?"

"Hi, Tracey . . . I wanted to really surprise you, but I chickened out and sent you the letter. You got it, right?"

Tracey walked over to him with a blank expression on her face. "What letter?"

"You know, the letter telling you I was coming home from Vietnam and would be coming down to visit you."

"Reggie, I'm sorry I . . . "

Before she could finish her sentence, Reggie leaned over and kissed her on the lips.

"Reggie, you can't do this."

"Why can't I?"

"Because you just can't just walk back into my life after a year. A year of not hearing from you and for the most part not knowing whether you were dead or alive."

Reggie became a little annoyed, stepped back, and said, "What do you mean not hearing from me? I wrote to you many times after I got to Vietnam, and not once did you answer my letters."

Tracey responded, "Letters? What letters? I never received any letters from you. You know why? Because you never wrote to me, Reggie!"

Reggie was taken aback. "I can't believe you are saying this, Tracey. You don't believe me?"

"Believe you? Why should I believe you? You never told me anything about you thinking about joining the Air Force. You were just here one day and gone the next. My parents always said you were . . . "

"I was what? Come on, Tracey, let's hear it!"

"Never mind. It's pointless now anyway."

He grabbed her gently by the arm and said, "Let's step outside for a moment."

He glanced over his shoulder and cocked his head as he observed Renee taking in the lively exchange. Tracey caught the gesture and followed him outside on to the porch of the sorority house. He leaned close to her and calmly said, "Tracey, you have to believe me. I did write to you . . . I did."

Tracey rolled her beautiful brown eyes that were now watery and pursed her lips. Reggie stood there in awe of her natural beauty. She hadn't gained a pound. She was still tall in stature. Her hair was so straight and laid ever so gently over her shoulders. Even at this moment, when she was obviously upset, her lips were so inviting and alluring. Reggie wanted to hold her and squeeze her and kiss her. He approached her once more, but she held her hands out, shook her head, and said, "No. Look, Reggie, a lot has happened since you left. When I didn't hear from you, I thought you didn't want me, and I ached all over for days. Finally, I got myself together when I came down here to school, and things are different now."

Reggie still couldn't believe what he was hearing. "So you don't believe me?"

Tracey shook her head and said, "I don't know what to believe, but it's too late, Reggie. We can't go back."

"Why not, Tracey? Why can't things be like they used to be?" Reggie's face brightened. He grabbed Tracey's arm, and said, "Look, I've been thinking about it for a long time. Why don't you come back with me?"

She pulled her arm away and said, "Back with you where?"

"Back to D.C. and then to California . . . San Francisco. I mentioned it in my last letter to you. I . . . "

She held up her hands and, with tears now streaming down her cheeks, said, "Reggie, I'm sorry, but that just can't happen right now. It's over. It's been over. Look, I'm sorry you drove all the way down here, but . . . "

Just then, a silver convertible sports car pulled up in front of the sorority house. A young man leaned over and yelled up to the occupants on the porch. "Tracey, you want me to park, or are you going to hop in?"

Tracey looked at Reggie, who turned to look at the stranger in the sports car. Tracey wiped her face, cleared her throat, and yelled over his shoulder, "Give me a minute, Clayton!"

Reggie was partially obstructing the stranger's view. He turned back to Tracey and asked the obvious, "Who's he?"

"His name is Clayton." Tracey hesitated. "Clayton Worthington and he's my boyfriend. I've been seeing him about eight months now."

Reggie took a small step back and looked deeply into her eyes before speaking. "So, that's the way it is, huh?"

Tracey stared back at him. "Yes, I'm sorry, Reggie, but that's the way it is. Look, I have to go. Have a wonderful life, Reginald Saunders."

She stepped around the now thoroughly stunned Reggie and headed off the porch to the awaiting car. The stranger leaned over and opened the door for her.

Reggie could hear him ask, "Who's that guy?"

He also heard Tracey's response: "Nobody."

CHAPTER 10

"**E**xcuse me, sir, would you like a snack? We should be arriving in approximately one hour."

Reggie Saunders looked up from his magazine and smiled at the stewardess. "Yes, thank you."

He placed the prepackaged meal on his seat tray and glanced out the window. Nothing but blue skies, sunshine, and white puffy clouds. He turned back and unraveled the cellophane around his food. The flight out from D.C. on the jetliner had been relatively smooth. He had slept for most of the six-hour flight. He had tried to think about the events of the past few weeks, starting with his abrupt departure from Hampton Roads, but it had been too painful. He had agonized over Tracey for several days. Even his family had noticed a certain degree of negativity and a major difference when he returned home that dreadful night. It was not a pleasant drive back up Interstate 95. He had wanted to bury himself someplace and let life pass him by. However, in another sense, he wanted to get on with his life and leave for California immediately. Anyway, he had stuck it out in D.C. for as long as he could. He had attempted to see a couple of old neighborhood buddies, his homeboys. But he found most were either in jail, shot, drugged out or, even worse, dead.

For a moment, he reflected on how he could have very well experienced a similar fate as some of his neighborhood friends. It wouldn't have taken much to go down that other path of crime and jail time. He was fortunate that he liked school and had always had good grades. His high school counselor, Mr. Holmes, always kept close tabs on him and encouraged him to maintain his studies. It was Mr. Holmes who had advised him to either attend college on the baseball scholarship that he was offered from a small college or join one of the Armed Forces.

He would say, "Just get off the streets, because they will eventually suck you into a life of crime and despair."

Reggie smiled as he fondly remembered all those after-school talks with Mr. Holmes. His mind switched to Tracey. He fought the thought. No, too painful. He thought he needed other women. But no, that didn't work either. The women he had contacted in an attempt to prove he still had it and was over Tracey proved to be uninteresting or too aggressive. They all seemed to have the attitude of "just show me your wallet, and let's get married, and then we might have sex." Of course, Reggie thought maybe he was his own worst enemy. Maybe it was like what one young lady had told him: he thought he was too good for any woman in the hood.

In any event, he had convinced himself to swear off any kind of committed relationship. From now on, it was going to be just sex. He finished his meal, reclined in his seat, and closed his eyes in preparation for his arrival in San Francisco.

CHAPTER 11

SAN FRANCISCO

Life and work had gone relatively easy for Airman Reginald Saunders. It had been almost a year since he stepped off the arriving flight to San Francisco. From the moment he walked down the ramp through the terminal and down to the baggage area, he felt exuberant and ready to take on the many challenges he knew would be coming. California at this point had truly lived up to its reputation of being a different world from the East Coast. It seemed every day was warm and sunny with little rain. The diverse group of people that he encountered—white, Hispanic, Asian—were all very friendly. He had met some blacks, but on the whole, just a few. It definitely wasn't like the East Coast, particularly D.C., where it seemed to him that everyone was black, except if you went down-town to the tourist areas. But California was different. Everyone seemed happy and had not a care in the world. It was definitely a free-spirited and happening place. Even Major Maxwell, his new boss, seemed like a regular, down-to-earth guy.

As he explored the base and experienced the calm, it was hard to believe that the nation was still at war halfway around the world. Major Maxwell had given him his assignment, explained all the procedures, and basically told him to listen, learn, and be available to drive him anywhere he needed to go on the base or in the city. In the interim, and with a lot of time off from his chauffeuring duties, Reggie had taken his old commander Lieutenant Colonel Rollins's advice and enrolled in classes at the nearby predominately-white community college.

Classes were going okay now, and the campus seemed to be settling down from Reggie's first day of registration. He remembered how he had taken the base military bus along with thirty or so other GIs over to the campus. What transpired after that was what Reggie thought nightmares were made of. As the bus pulled on campus, hundreds of students (and not a black face in the crowd), in protest of the Vietnam War, converged on the bus and pelted it with fruits, eggs, and rotten vegetables. Many of the white students held anti-Vietnam War signs and shouted obscenities at the occupants on the bus. Reggie and the rest of the young men were startled and confused. The entire scene was scary and demoralizing. Here, he and the rest of the men had just returned from Vietnam—a nasty war, where young men the ages of many of these protestors were fighting and dying for their country—only to return home to be ridiculed and lambasted in public. He could only shake his head as he peered out the slush-stained windows and hoped that the bus driver would get through the mob of students without running any of them over.

The campus police had quickly restored order and the incident was reported in all the local newspapers. He learned later that many college campuses across the country went through similar student protest of the Vietnam War on that unforgettable day. The dean of the college had apologized to each of the GIs and welcomed them on campus. But some-how his apologies didn't suppress the inner anger of the men and their confusion as to why America's youth had taken on an all-out assault on the United States government.

The base commander, once he heard about the incident, sent out a memo to all military personnel to be cautious when moving in and about town. Even Major Maxwell suggested to Reggie that he was happy he had decided to take classes at the local college, but he should seriously consider wearing civilian clothes while on campus to avoid any unnecessary altercations. Reggie agreed that it was a good idea and made it a point to wear attire that blended in on campus after his military duties.

That was a year ago. Today, he had just gotten off his military shift and was in between classes. He was walking down the hallway of the campus Administration Building when he noticed a group of guys standing in front of a bulletin board. The gathering of young men piqued his interest. So he walked over to see what was going on. They were all reading a notice for try-outs for the Intramural League Baseball Team. He stepped closer to read the details and thought about the possibility of playing baseball again. He determined that the times for practice and games wouldn't interfere with his military assignment or classes. The thought of baseball made him smile. He knew he needed the challenge, so he made up his mind to check out the first practice.

CHAPTER 12

"Well, I can't believe I'm in the great mystery apartment of the one and only Mr. Morris Whitehead."

Sheila Montrose entered the dimly-lit living room. Morris had already entered the apartment and had rushed through several strands of hanging multi-colored beads leading down the hallway to his bedroom. He wanted to make sure everything was in place.

He called back, "Believe it, and make yourself at home. I'll be with you in a minute."

Sheila took off her coat and laid it on one of the leather chairs in front of her. She looked to her left and saw the kitchen area with its cute little table for two. She briefly walked into the kitchen, and as she expected, everything was neat and clean. No dirty dishes in the sink. She thought about peeking in the refrigerator but decided against it. She walked out of the kitchen and headed across the living room to the balcony's sliding glass doors and stepped out. Morris was coming down the hallway. She leaned over the balcony railing and admired the city street lights beneath her. Morris saw her as he approached.

"How do you like it?"

Sheila turned, smiled, and said, "Nice view. I like what I've seen so far."

Morris saw her smile and said, "Well, the most important room is down the hallway. Let's step inside because the personal guided tour starts about now."

He grabbed her hand and guided her back into the apartment.

She quickly dislodged her hand and said, "Not so fast, Mr. White-head. I need to know what made you invite me up to your apartment?"

Morris shook his head and asked, "What do you mean?"

"Well, I mean from what I've gathered from all the women at work whom you've dated, no one has ever been to your apartment."

"Whoa, whoa, all what women at work?"

"Oh, come on, Morris. Women talk, and you do have a reputation as a ladies' man."

Morris thought for a moment about how he might maneuver his way around this particular dilemma. He decided that when in doubt, although it might kill the mood, honesty was usually the best policy. "Look, Sheila, we've been out on a few dates now, and I like you. I like you a lot. So this is what I think guys do when they like someone. They invite them up to their apartment." He hunched his shoulders.

"And that's about it. As for all the so-called other women, well, that's exactly the way I see it—so-called."

He sensed that he might be breaking the ice, so he quickly shifted gears and grabbed her hand again while saying, "Hey, dinner was great, wasn't it?"

Sheila nodded, and Morris added as he was still admiring her beautiful brown eyes, milk chocolate complexion, and perfectly-styled Afro hair, "So let's just continue to enjoy the evening and . . . say, how about a drink?"

Sheila nodded once again as Morris quickly ushered her to the sofa that faced the glass doors of the balcony. Feeling comfortable that she would stay put for a moment, he stepped across the room to his stereo wall and pushed the button on his Teac reel-to-reel tape deck. He needed mood music fast.

Smokey Robinson kicked in with his soulful lyrics to "Fork in the Road." Morris crossed his fingers as he headed to the kitchen to open a bottle of wine.

He called out, "I hope you like Riunite?"

"That's fine." She continued to observe the apartment. It was indeed nice and in a great section of the city. She noticed a photo album among all the *Ebony* and *Jet* magazines on the glass coffee table in front of her. She called out to Morris, "This is a pretty photo album. I like the unique leather binding . . . looks special. Are they family photos?"

Morris brought out the wine and answered, "No, just a collection of photos of a lot of things."

"Do you mind if I look?"

"No, go ahead."

She looked through the various photographs as Morris joined her. He poured wine in each of the glasses and gave one to her. He held his glass up in front of him, indicating a toast. Sheila raised her glass and clinked his.

Morris smiled and said, "To us."

Sheila nodded and took a sip of the wine as she looked deeply into his eyes. Her heart raced, and her mind was doing double time. She wanted to fight her feelings for this man. She knew of some of his escapades but somehow felt things were different when they were together. He always made her feel special and that she was the only one. The only thing that made sense to her at this moment was that she was in his apartment and asking herself, *Is this for real or what?*

She returned her glass on the coffee table and flipped a few more pages in the album. She came upon what she thought was an interesting photograph of two men in military combat gear.

"Who's this?" she asked, pointing to one of the men.

Morris put down his glass and leaned forward. "Oh, that's Reggie Saunders, and that's me," he said, pointing to the other young man. "That's a picture of us when we were in Vietnam."

"Cute."

"Me or Reggie?"

She laughed, "Well, both. So where's Reggie now?"

Morris picked up his glass and took a sip before replying. "Actually, I'm not sure. We sort of lost track of each other after we came back from

Vietnam. He was heading for D.C. That's where he's from. Then he was going to go out to California. So I guess he could be in either place."

Sheila leaned back on the sofa and was closer to Morris.

"You guys look pretty close in that picture."

"Yeah, we were really close, especially near the end of our tour. We had a lot of good times and a few scary times, but we made it."

Morris held his glass and stared out the balcony doors. "Yeah, we were supposed to hook up after we got back, but you know how it goes. You know, going to write, going to call, going to visit—never happens. I guess he went his way, and I went mine. We both got busy with our lives and hey . . ."

She pointed to another photograph and asked, "And these Asian-looking ladies you are with?"

Morris leaned forward and closed the album, not responding. Sheila didn't know what quite to make of his gesture but sensed he was deeply moved. She decided it wasn't worth pursuing any further. She changed the subject. "So what's this I've been hearing about you and a transfer?"

Morris smiled. "Wow, news travels fast, doesn't it?"

"Well?"

"Well, it may happen. I'm not sure."

He looked at Sheila and could see the determination in her face. He knew she wasn't going to let the subject go. He had known for weeks that he was being transferred. But he definitely didn't want to discuss it on this night for fear of running her off and face the possibility of sleeping alone. For it was true that he had dated many women, but Sheila was special. He honestly wanted to get to know her better. The thought had occurred to him that maybe he was slowing down—maybe he was getting soft. So he was perplexed as to whether he should take the chance and be honest—for once. He made up his mind to go for it.

"Okay, okay, how can I refuse those great big, beautiful, brown eyes? Yes, I'm being transferred."

He hesitated and looked for a reaction. Sheila kept her poise.

He continued, "I'm going to headquarters in Detroit. . . "

Still no reaction from her.

"I report next month."

Sheila raised her glass and slowly took a sip of wine. Smokey's seductive rendition of "Ooo Baby Baby" was wafting through the speakers in the background. Morris got up and held his hand out to her. She returned her glass on the coffee table and got up to follow him. He led her down the hallway and parted the red beads guarding the entrance to his bedroom. She hesitated and pulled his hand back.

"Morris, I don't want to be just another conquest."

As he released the beads behind her, he leaned over, kissed her softly, and said, "Baby, I promise. . . you won't be."

CHAPTER 13

SAN FRANCISCO

Coach Jim Hamilton held his clipboard in front of him and glanced down at the names and positions on the signup sheet. Twenty or so young men sat on the grass in front of him and awaited their instructions. Coach Hamilton looked up, adjusted his baseball cap, and pulled his trousers up over his potbelly before speaking. "Well, this looks like an interesting group. It seems everyone wants to play in the outfield. Of course, gentlemen, you all know that can't happen because baseball doesn't have twenty outfield positions."

Some of the young men laughed at what was construed to be a joke from the coach.

Coach Hamilton continued, "So, I guess one thing I'm going to do is assign some other positions. But first, I want to say a few words about what this whole intramural baseball is all about. It is purely voluntary. This is not the Majors, gentlemen. This is not the Minors, Triple-A, Double-A, not even a four-year state college baseball program. It's just a means to provide extracurricular activity at the tax payers' expense in sports for those who are interested in participating. So you can look around and see there are no grandstands with hundreds of cheering people. The playing fields are adequate, but they won't be Candlestick

Park. My job is to hopefully keep us competitive with other junior colleges in the state and to have a little fun in the process.

"However . . ." He paused. "Having said all that, I will ask and demand 100 percent effort from each of you while you are practicing and on the playing field. Now does anyone have a problem with that?" The coach looked down. No one objected to his rhetorical question. He continued, "Okay, so the first thing we are going to do is go through some basic drills so that I can, shall we say, reassign some of you outfielders to other positions. Also, I want the people . . ." He glanced at his clipboard again. "The people who signed up for pitchers . . . Starks; Pruzenski; Saunders; and the catcher, Lomax. Lomax, where are you?"

A sandy-blond-haired young man raised his hand.

"Okay, Lomax, go over there with the pitchers and see Assistant Coach Jamison."

He pointed to the assistant coach several feet away. As Lomax, Starks, Pruzenski, and Reggie got up to go over to the assistant coach, Coach Hamilton glanced over his clipboard at Reggie and said, "And you are?"

Reggie didn't quite know what to make of the question. The first thing that raced through his mind was: *Okay, so I'm the only black guy here. So here comes the prejudice. But better play it safe for now.* He answered the coach. "I'm Saunders, coach."

Coach Hamilton eyed Reggie up and down closely. "And you are a pitcher?"

There were a few chuckles from the remaining group. Reggie looked over at Starks and Pruzenski, both of whom stood over six feet and probably weighed in the 200-pounds range. Reggie paled in comparison at 5'10" and 150 pounds soaking wet. But he managed to respond, "Yeah, coach, I'm a pitcher."

Coach Hamilton shook his head, still somewhat doubtful, and said, "Okay, Saunders, in due time we'll see what you've got." He called over to Lomax and said, "Get in gear and let these guys alternate throwing to you." He turned to the remaining group, blew his whistle, and yelled, "Practice begins now, gentlemen!"

Three hours passed as the spring sunshine and accompanying warmth took its toll on most of the out-of-shape athletes. Reggie had alternated throwing with Starks and Pruzenski, who both seemed to be tiring. He hadn't especially felt tired. He actually felt good and was now throwing in a rhythm. Maybe that stint in Vietnam and enduring the constant and sweltering heat had helped him more than he ever realized. The other surprising thing was that Lomax had been catching everything that he had thrown. Although he purposely didn't throw hard, all his changeups and curves didn't appear to bother Lomax. Not even his patented "slow-drop ball." The one that he threw straight down the pike and would drop, as if off a dining room table, just as it reached the plate. His catchers always had a problem handling that pitch, but not Lomax.

Lomax kept yelling back to Reggie, "Hey, Saunders. When are you going to bring the heat?"

Reggie smiled, but he never answered the question. There was something he liked about Lomax. He seemed to be a genuine kind of guy.

Coach Hamilton wiped his brow with his handkerchief, looked at his watch, signaled his assistant to halt practice, and blew his whistle.

"Alright, men. That's it for today. I'll see you tomorrow, same time, same place."

The young men picked up their gear and dispersed. Coach Hamilton watched as the pitchers and catcher gathered their things and headed toward the parking lot. He approached his assistant, Jamison. "Well, what do you think?"

Jamison removed his baseball cap, wiped his forehead with his sweaty arm, shrugged, and replied, "Not bad, coach. I've seen worse."

"How about that Saunders kid?"

"Well, he's not especially fast. I don't know whether he was holding back, though. But he's got a real deceptive, slow curve ball that breaks down right to left. I also saw him throw a few off-pace fastballs that seemed to drop just before they reached the plate." Jamison continued, "For a small guy, he can be surprisingly smooth and accurate. He can definitely get the ball across the plate."

Coach Hamilton shook his head. "Well, now, that surprises me." He slapped his assistant on the back. "Hey, well, let's get out of here; it's been a long day."

Reggie was headed across the field toward the bus stop when Lomax ran up behind him and called out, "Hey, Saunders, you need a ride back to base?"

Reggie turned, somewhat surprised, and looked at Lomax. "You're going back to base?"

Lomax extended his hand. "Yep, Airman McArthur Lomax at your service."

"Well, I'll be damned. I thought I was the only service guy there today. How did you know? Or better yet, why didn't you say something before now?"

"You just had that swagger about you, and what did you want me to say?"

"Hell, I don't know—just something to let me know we were in this together."

"I don't know, Saunders. We seemed to click without the formal introduction."

Reggie started to walk alongside Lomax and observed that he was about the same height, but Lomax was much stouter—almost chunky. Catching definitely suited his build. He extended his hand and said, "Airman Reginald Saunders. Where in the hell did you get that first name—McArthur?"

Lomax laughed. "Yeah, everybody asks me that. My father was a big fan of General Douglas McArthur. I guess it could have been worse. He could have named me Douglas. I don't think I would have liked the nickname Doug. So just call me Mac, okay?"

Reggie replied, "Okay, you got it, and thanks for the ride offer, Mac."

As they threw their gear into Mac's green 61 Ford Fairlane, Reggie remarked, "Nice wheels, man."

Lomax nodded and said, "Thanks."

As Mac pulled out of the parking lot, Reggie looked over and said, "So, where you from, Mac?"

Mac looked over at Reggie and smiled, "Idaho . . . Boise, Idaho."

"You are joking, right? Cause nobody's from Idaho."

"Nope, no joke. I was born and raised on a farm. You'll like this . . . a potato farm."

Reggie shook his head. "No way, man."

"Hey, somebody's got to supply the military and McDonald's with all those potatoes and French fries."

They both laughed. Reggie settled in the passenger seat and momentarily glanced out the window and admired the glimmering sun sinking slowly in the west. How he loved the California days. He turned back to Mac. "So tell me, Mac. How did you wind up in the Air Force?"

Mac smiled and responded, "Well, it's really no big deal. I grew up on the farm and just got tired of picking potatoes. An Air Force recruiter came to my high school and convinced me and a couple of other guys from my town that if we joined up, we would see the world. So I did. Haven't seen much of the world, but this part of the country isn't too bad—especially for an old farm boy like me. California is crazy cool, man, and I was able to avoid Vietnam."

Reggie nodded and said, "Yeah," under his breath. He managed to change the subject. "So how'd you get into baseball?"

Mac shrugged. "Hell, everybody plays baseball where I'm from. It's our favorite pastime. We start out in grade school and play right through high school and college if we are good enough. I could have gone on to college, but as I said, I wanted to see the world." He laughed and continued, "So I'm taking a few classes here at the college." Mac looked back to Reggie. "So, what about you, Saunders, or can I call you by your first name?"

"Oh, me, yeah, call me Reggie." Reggie told Mac a little about his early childhood growing up in the hood of D.C. and more about his experience in Vietnam. He had just finished his story about the foxhole and "Charlie" overrunning the perimeter of the base and how he and his band of merry men were called upon to defend it. He didn't mention the shooting of the cows incident. He had decided on the plane back from Vietnam that the story played better without bringing that part up.

Mac was riveted by Reggie's experience in Vietnam. As he pulled up to the military barracks, his face was expressionless. He put his car in park and turned to Reggie. "Man, that was one hell of a story. You must have been scared shitless."

Reggie shook his head. "Naw," he lied. "It was all in a day's work. Hey, but I'm glad to be back."

They both sat there for a moment before Mac said, "Hey, look, Reggie, if you want, you can ride with me tomorrow after practice."

Reggie pulled his gear out of the backseat. "That would be great, Mac, and thanks again. I'll see you tomorrow."

CHAPTER 14

The coach representing the home team walked behind home plate and the protective metal fencing around the batter's cage to approach Coach Hamilton. He studied his score sheet before speaking. "Coach, I've got bottom of the ninth, and you are ahead three to two."

Coach Hamilton looked at his clipboard and checked his score sheet. "That's what I've got, coach."

The home plate umpire yelled, "Batter up!"

As the opposing coach walked back to the third-base side of the field, he stopped momentarily and talked to his batter in the on-deck circle. On the other side of the field, Coach Hamilton paced in front of his bench of players. He looked out onto the field to the pitcher's mound and nodded to Starks. Lomax caught Starks's final practice pitch and fired the ball to the third baseman, who in turn started the formal throwing rotation around the infield to second base, first base, and then back to Starks on the mound.

Coach Hamilton took a deep breath and glanced down the first base side of the field to his assistant, Jamison. Before the beginning of the inning, they had discussed whether to leave Starks in to pitch the final inning or bring in Pruzenski or Saunders. Jamison had suggested a relief pitcher, possibly Saunders, since Pruzenski had pitched the previous game and was a little sore. Jamison mentioned to the coach that Saunders had warmed up and looked good. Coach Hamilton still wasn't quite sold on Saunders's ability, especially in this critical situation. The team had already lost their first two games, and he shuddered at the thought of going zero to three, especially now that they were in the lead. All they had to do was to hold on. He decided he would stick with Starks.

Five minutes later, Coach Hamilton realized that it was not the right decision. Starks walked the first batter, and the second batter tagged him for a homerun over the left-field fence. Final score was four to three in favor of the opposing team.

As the players shook hands and walked back to their buses, Mac ran up to Reggie and said, "I told Jamison to put you in, but I guess he didn't convince Coach Hamilton."

Reggie was a little dejected, but he managed to say, "Hey, that's the way it goes. It's only a game. I'll get my chance one day."

Mac slapped Reggie on the back and said, "See? That's what I really like about you. Nothing seems to faze you."

Reggie smiled in apparent agreement. They got on the bus and sat down beside each other as they headed back to school. After they were on their way, Mac turned to Reggie and said, "Say, why don't you hang out with me tonight? I'm going to a party across the bridge over in Sausalito."

Reggie thought for a moment before replying. "Hell, why not. It's Friday. I'm done for the week, and hey, this is California, right?"

"Right, man. I'll drop you off at your barrack to shower and then swing back to pick you up."

CHAPTER 15

When Reggie returned home to D.C. from Vietnam, he had made a point to go to the library and find out all he could about California, particularly San Francisco. Researching San Francisco felt like old times and reminded him of his childhood when he would visit the big library downtown, spending hours reading books. A lot of the time was spent on homework assignments, but whatever the assignment, he had always dug in and researched the topic to the max. He also made a point to check out books to take home to read—books on faraway places and countries, books on art that interested him. Although he never had an interest in painting or anything, he always seemed to gravitate to books with paintings and drawings by artists like Van Gogh, Renoir, or Degas.

At the library, he had read several books that had described the Golden Gate Bridge, but none of them did justice to the magnificently-engineered structure. He was completely in awe as he eyed the massive steel expansion girders and the guardrails protecting vehicles and pedestrians from plummeting hundreds of feet into the cold, murky waters of the San Francisco Bay. Mac punched his four-speed Hurst stick shift into third gear before snatching it into fourth. The Ford Fairlane jumped as it sped across the bridge.

Twenty minutes later, they were ascending several winding streets leading up to a well-lit A-frame home nestled in the hills of Sausalito. They could hear the music blaring long before they reached the circular driveway of the home. As they drove up, Reggie was impressed. "Nice pad."

Mac smiled, "Yeah, it's pretty nice. Belongs to one of my friend's parents who are out of town. So let's party, my good buddy."

An attractive and slim brunette who introduced herself as Paulette greeted them at the door. Mac and Reggie stepped in and immediately headed for the bar that was set up through the giant, glass, double doors leading to the patio and a gigantic swimming pool. Reggie reached into a large, icy, beer tub and pulled out two Budweisers. He handed one to Mac as he admired the view and the scantily-clad women sitting around the pool. A few more people arrived, and someone cranked up the 8-track tape player even louder. "Louie Louie" resonated throughout the home and onto the outside patio.

After eyeing Paulette once again, Mac raised his beer can to Reggie and said, "Partner, you are on your own. Talk to you later."

Reggie acknowledged Mac's abrupt departure, took a swig of beer, and scoped out the revelers who were now dancing around the pool and also in what must have been a living room or family area. He went inside and quickly observed that all the women dancing were white. He looked around the room and observed he was the only person of color there. He was somewhat uneasy because he had never socially been around white folks, especially white women, in his life. They certainly were not in the hood of the northeast section of D.C. where he grew up. Other than seeing white women on TV, the movies, or in magazines, they weren't in his neighborhood, nor had they existed in his early childhood or adolescent world. Not that he was prejudiced or anything, because his mother had always taught him and his siblings that they should look past the color of a person's skin. People of all colors were God's children. Thus far, he had subscribed to those teachings, albeit with little opportunity to practice them. It just never seemed to come up. The blacks sort of stayed in their all-black world, and the whites, for all Reggie knew, stayed in their all-white world. However, since he had sworn off any committed relationship with a woman since Tracey, he felt if the opportunity presented itself, he would date and explore all persuasions of women. He further thought to himself, *After all, this is California, land of many shades of women, particularly tanned.*

He continued to stand in one place or another around the room. Women passed by him, and a few of them smiled and said, "Hi."

He politely returned the greetings. Now that he was in this situation, he was still confused as to what he should do. He felt he couldn't draw on his recent experiences on how to act at a party. He had been to a couple of predominantly-black parties since he had been in California. They had proved to be negative experiences as far as he was concerned. Another nail in the coffin of why women—black women—never seemed to notice him. After Tracey, his social life had just seemed to go downhill as far as black women were concerned.

He remembered how in every one of those parties he attended, he would make the effort to be sociable to meet a nice-looking sister. And invariably, they would politely or even worse, rudely, ignore him. Most of the time, he couldn't even get a good dance in. He would walk all the way across a room to ask a woman to dance, and they would look at him as if he had a sign on that said, "Hi, I'm a real jerk."

And they would say, "No, thanks"—almost all the time.

The few who did dance with him always made it seem like they were doing him a big favor. And never once had he gotten to the point of getting a telephone number. Some of his brothers back on base would joke with him and said his problem stemmed from the fact that he didn't have a line. He would always ask, "How do you get a line?" Of course, his so-called brothers would just laugh louder.

He concluded that his "meet them, date them, make love to them, and make no commitment to them" posture hadn't quite worked out thus far, but he would keep trying. He took another swig of beer and decided to down the whole can. Chug-a-lug. This made him feel better as he felt a little buzz coming on. It also gave him the confidence to admit to himself that he was perfectly objective in his rationalization that he and black women still had a long way to go. But for now, the question before him was how to maintain his color blindness in this new white arena? The ways, the means, the whys of the black/white world would have to be solved by someone else.

He grabbed another Budweiser from a beer cooler on the patio and popped the can. He walked back into the dancing area. All the people on the floor were getting down to Kool & the Gang. He instinctively swayed to the beat. He may not have had a line, but he was convinced that he had rhythm.

The sea of bobbing heads briefly reminded him of the time he was in Hong Kong. Of course, the women there weren't white, but then again, they weren't black either. Reggie thought further. Those Asian babes might as well have been black. He remembered how they were up on all the latest black happenings. They dressed like sisters, spoke the black ghetto slang, and loved soul music. He never missed a beat with those Asian women in Hong Kong. It felt like being back home in D.C. the entire time he was there. But that was then. Here he was now looking at a room full of beautiful, tanned women. Most could pass for models in his book. He pulled another beer from a cooler, took a deep breath, and pondered his predicament further.

He finally concluded that it actually didn't matter to him that he was at this particular party. The problem was that he wasn't sure of the women's reaction to him. He certainly didn't want to make an ass of himself by asking one of them to dance only to have them say no, because then he would have to ask himself some hard questions: did they say no because they just didn't want to dance? Or did they say no because he was black? He didn't like his options, so he decided that he would sit this one out, that is, take in a little more of the scenery, drink a couple more beers, find Mac, convince him to leave, and then make a graceful exit.

He walked over to the far corner of the room where he decided he would stand next to a cactus plant and become inconspicuous. He glanced to his left and saw another brother at the front door. He recognized him as a basketball player from the college, but he couldn't remember his name. The basketball player noticed him and nodded as he worked his way across the dance area. A gorgeous blonde walked over to him and hugged and kissed him. Reggie relaxed as he stood by the plant.

He had not been standing by the cactus plant long before an attractive young lady approached him. He had noticed her coming in his direction through the crowd of partygoers. His first inclination was to turn and look behind him. Of course, there was nothing behind him but a wall. Although he had downed a couple more beers, the cactus plant had not made some miraculous transformation into a human being standing next to him, so he sucked in his stomach as she approached.

"Hi, aren't you one of the new players on Clairemont's Basketball Team?"

Reggie was in awe of how attractive she was. He pretended to take a drink from his now-empty beer can. "Uh, hi. No, I'm not on the basketball team. I'm here with a friend." He looked over her shoulder to point Mac out, but he apparently was in another room. When the woman looked a little confused and somewhat embarrassed, realizing she had obviously made a mistake, Reggie quickly added, "But I am on the baseball team at Clairemont."

She smiled and extended her hand. "Oh, I'm sorry. I'm Barbara, but my friends call me Barbie."

A million thoughts raced through Reggie's mind as to what to say. A little voice up there somewhere said, *Use a line; use a line. Something, man, anything. It's either now or never—so go for it you, idiot!*

He put on his electric smile. The one that he always gave thanks and credit to the Air Force for giving him. He could say lots of good thing about the Air Force. One of the best things he could say was their dental plan. It took them over a year, but the military dentists had worked a miracle on his teeth. They straightened and whitened the hell out of Reggie's teeth. After they were through, he could have posed for a national poster advertisement. In this do or die moment only one name came to his mind. He took Barbie's hand, kissed it, and coolly said, "Hi, I'm Silk, and my friends call me Silk."

Clearly taken aback, but intrigued by his response and smile, she slowly removed her hand from his gentle grasp and replied, "Oh, really now? That's an unusual name." She smiled, hesitated, and continued. "It, shall we say, brings a lot of connotations to mind. So why do they call you Silk?"

Reggie sat his empty can down in the cactus plant, took Barbie's hand once again, and guided her to the middle of the dance area. The Righteous Brothers' "Unchained Melody" was playing. He pulled her close to him and softly replied, "Let's just see," all the while thinking to himself, *What the hell did I just say?*

CHAPTER 16

The umpire yelled, "Batter up!"

Coach Hamilton paced in front of his team sitting on the first base side of the playing field. He pondered his now-familiar predicament. His team was ahead of their opponent and only needing a final push and a little luck to close out the game. It was the bottom of the ninth inning, and Pruzenski was on the mound throwing his final practice pitch. He had pitched a good game but appeared to be tiring. Still, the score was six-five in favor of Clairemont. The coach looked across the field to the third-base side. He locked eyes with Jamison, who nodded. The coach pondered for another moment. He looked down the bench at Reggie. Then he yelled to the umpire, "Time out, ump!" He briskly headed for the pitcher's mound.

The umpire held his hands out and repeated, "Time out." He too approached the pitcher's mound.

The opposing team's coach yelled at the ump. "Come on, ump. What the hell is going on? Delay of game, delay of game!"

Coach Hamilton said something quickly to Pruzenski, who handed him the ball and left the mound. The coach signaled for Reggie, who grabbed his glove and dashed toward the mound. The ump, Mac, the coach, and now Reggie converged on the mound. The opposing coach was still yelling, "Play ball. Let's play ball!"

The umpire spoke to Coach Hamilton. "Look, coach, you had sufficient time between innings to make a change in pitchers."

The coach responded, "Yeah, I know, ump, but I changed my mind."

The ump looked at him and said, "You know, I could call you for delay of game, but since we are having so much fun here…" He looked over at the now-livid opposing coach. "I'll stretch the rule if your man is ready to go right now—and I mean now with no practice pitches."

The coach looked at Reggie and then at Mac who winked and said, "He's ready, ump."

Coach Hamilton handed Reggie the ball and said, "Let's go get them, son."

Mac looked at Reggie and simply added, "It's the big dance now, partner—just follow my lead."

The umpire looked at his watch and yelled, "Let's play ball and batter up!" over the opposing coach who was still protesting.

Reggie took a deep breath and went through his routine of palming the rosin bag and then pounding the ball three times in his glove for good luck. He felt fairly relaxed because he had warmed up a little behind the bench prior to being called in by Coach Hamilton. He settled his cleats on the pitching rubber atop the mound and leaned forward to face the batter. He exhaled while saying to himself, *Okay, okay, it's now or never.* He watched for Mac to give him a sign.

The first two pitches to the batter were balls. Coach Hamilton started to pace again. Mac stood up and partially walked in front of the batter to throw the ball back to Reggie. He motioned and called out as he threw, "Slow it down. Slow it down."

The next pitch was a strike, as the batter was obviously signaled by his coach to take the pitch. The count was two balls and one strike. *So now the fun begins*, Reggie thought as he went through his windup.

The pitch was popped up to the infield, and the second baseman had no problem making the catch. One out. After a couple of called balls and three foul balls, the next batter hit a ball deep to left field. It was caught, however, just prior to the fence. Two outs. Reggie walked the next batter on four straight pitches that were called balls by the ump. The next batter approached the plate. Mac signaled to the ump that he wanted a time-out. He headed toward the mound.

Coach Hamilton started to walk out, but he looked over to Jamison, who held his thumb up, indicating that his pitcher was okay. Mac stood alone with Reggie on the mound.

"This guy is one of their best hitters, and we really get into the meat of the lineup after him. So we can't make any mistakes. Let's keep him off balance with your slow stuff. Just watch where I place my mitt. Nothing over the plate because he'll annihilate it, okay, Silk?"

Reggie smiled as he thought that it had been a while since he had heard "Silk" in conjunction with a baseball game. Mac had heard him use it a couple of times when Reggie was talking to women. It had become a tall tale between the two. Mac dropped the ball in Reggie's glove and headed for home plate.

The first pitch to the batter was a called ball. The next pitch was lined down the third base side but was foul. Reggie allowed the runner on first base too much lead, and on the next pitch, he stole second base. Mac made a gallant effort to throw him out, but the lead was too much to overcome even with his arm and accuracy. Mac shook his head and motioned to Reggie that it was okay. No harm, just concentrate on the batter.

The inning seemed like an eternity, but the count finally stood at three balls and two strikes. Mac signaled several pitches to Reggie, but Reggie shook all of them off. He knew what pitch he wanted to throw. He took his partial windup and threw some heat. A fastball right down the middle of the plate. The ball had so much speed that it was practically in Mac's catcher's mitt before the batter could get his bat around. The swoosh of the bat and the popping sound of Mac's mitt were unbelievably loud. Swing and a miss—strike three! Game over! Clairemont's entire bench emptied and rushed on to the field to congratulate Reggie. Everyone realized that they had won their first baseball game. The forty or so fans in the makeshift stands, many of them women, cheered their excitement and approval.

Mac was the first to reach Reggie. "Where the hell did that last pitch come from? My hand is still stinging."

Reggie shook his head, smiled, and said, "I've been saving it especially for you, good buddy."

They both laughed as the rest of the team, coaches, and fans joined them.

They were in a festive mood as they headed to the parking lot and the team bus. Mac turned to Reggie.

"Hey, you going to join us at Elmo's Bar tonight?"

"Wouldn't miss it for the world."

"Great, my car is back at the barracks. I'll pick you up at 19:00."

"Nope, I'm picking you up tonight."

Mac stopped and looked at Reggie before repeating what he had just heard. "You are going to pick me up?"

"Yep."

"In what, pray tell?"

"In that."

They had reached the parking lot, and Reggie pointed to a shiny, deep, dark maroon 65 Ford Mustang fastback. Mac rushed over to the car and circled it. "When the hell did you get this?"

"Picked it up earlier today. Thought it was about time I got something to match my new image. Might enhance my love life." He pulled a handkerchief from his pocket, knelt down, and wiped a water spot off one of the custom chrome Mag wheels. "We're going to ride in style tonight. Not that your car isn't style."

Mac stood there with his mouth open before saying, "Man, this is definitely a sweet ride. I wondered why you weren't on the team bus coming to the game."

Reggie slapped him on the back and said, "Throw your stuff in the back and hop in. I got permission from Coach Hamilton. It's all good, man. We'll catch up with the guys." He pointed to several women headed for their cars and in their direction. "And our admiring fans later."

He slipped in an 8-track tape of "Move Your Hand" by Lonnie Liston Smith, turned up the volume, and slowly pulled out of the parking lot. He wanted to make sure the approaching women heard the music, saw the car, and noticed who was in it.

CHAPTER 17

California, California, California. That's all Reggie could say to himself as he sat in the small hallway just outside Major Maxwell's office. Life in the Golden State had certainly been good to him. His classes at school had gone great. He had taken and passed all his finals and was due to graduate with his associate's degree in less than a month. The baseball team had finished their season with a flurry. They had won enough games to finish third in the league and qualified for the play-offs, which they ultimately lost in the semi-final round. His individual record was four-zero with an additional two saves. He had become a living legend of sorts. Mac and he were still the best of friends, taking advantage of their celebrity status on campus with every woman they met. He quickly learned, and Mac too, that when he borrowed the Mustang, the car just automatically drew women to it and its occupant. He never anticipated it, but even though it was baseball instead of the more popular basketball or football, he was enjoying the athlete's lifestyle of endless parties, sex, booze, and marijuana. If there were a downside, "exhausting" would be the word to use. The Silk line worked 99.9 percent of the time. He had been with so many women that he could hardly remember their names. He had truly lived up to the "Silk" image and kept his vow to stay uncommitted. His military assignment had been most rewarding and did not interfere with all the other things going on in his seemingly hectic and carefree life. He was indeed living the dream.

So there he was waiting to see Major Maxwell about another cross-road in his young life fast. His four-year military obligation was just about up, and he had to make a decision as to whether he would reenlist or get out of the Air Force and take his chances in the real world. He had thought long and hard about it. Plus, he and Mac had talked about it extensively. Mac's time was about up, too. He had already made his decision to get out. His plans were to return home to Boise to his family and the potato farm and finish the remainder of college. Mac had been apologetic and persuasive in telling Reggie not to let his decision to go back to Boise influence Reggie's own decision to go or stay. Although Reggie valued their friendship, he assured Mac that it would be his personal decision on whatever he decided to do.

What he didn't tell Mac, however, was that he had had no clue as to what he was going to do until the day before, when he attended a job fair on campus. A recruiter for a car company back east, D.C. to be exact, had spoken to him and suggested he go back east for an interview. As much as he loved California, the sunshine, the carefree lifestyle, and the women, he knew it was a gamble, because the recruiter didn't guarantee the job. However, the thought of going back home to D.C. was too tempting. He felt it had to be an omen of some kind.

Major Maxwell stepped out of his office. Reggie stood and saluted. The major saluted and motioned for him to come in and sit down. The major picked up a file on his desk. Reggie presumed it was his.

"Airman Saunders, it looks like your first four years in the Air Force is just about up. I'm supposed to give you a long spiel as to why reenlisting would be in your best interest. But having personally worked with you for almost two years now, I wanted to first say thank you for a job well done. I have to admit I was quite surprised at your ability to handle everything I threw at you. Not to mention the fact that you managed to complete two years of college. I wrote Lieutenant Colonel Rollins and told him he finally got something right and how pleased I've been with your performance."

The major smiled. Reggie nodded in acknowledgment but wondered where the major was headed with the discussion.

"Which brings me to my final thought. Frankly, Saunders, I personally feel that you are intelligent and a born leader. You could make it in any arena. Of course, we'd like you to stay in the Air Force. As a matter of fact, I would personally recommend you for Officer Candidate School. All you would have to do is pass the exam, which I'm sure you are capable of doing. The only downside, if you will, is that you commit to Uncle Sam for five years your next hitch instead of four years." The major leaned back in his chair, closed the file, and simply added, "So it's really your call, airman."

Reggie rustled a little in his chair as he took in what the major had just said to him. Never in his wildest dreams could he have imagined being recommended to Officer Candidate School and having the opportunity to be giving the orders rather than receiving them. The offer really intrigued him. However, he had made up his mind. He cleared his throat before responding to the major.

"Well sir, I'm definitely thankful and honored that you would recommend me to Officer Candidate School. And I really like the Air Force. I've met so many wonderful people and learned so many things, things and experiences that I'll remember for the rest of my life." Reggie hesitated before continuing. "But I've been offered a job opportunity to return home to Washington, D.C." He shook his head. "And I feel I just can't pass up on it. So I've decided I'm going to get out."

The major seemed to understand. He nodded his head and said, "Well, I can't blame you, and I wish you the very best. I'll expedite your discharge papers, and I hope to be reading or hearing good things about you one day." He rose from his desk and extended his hand to Reggie. "Good luck, airman."

Reggie threw his duffel bag in the back of the Mustang. Then he stepped around the car to say goodbye to Mac. He shook hands and hugged him. "Goodbye, old buddy. I'm going to really miss you."

Mac stepped back from the embrace and said, "Yeah." He smiled and added, "Silk, I'm going to miss you. too. But we'll stay in touch, right?"

Reggie slapped him on the shoulder and returned to the driver's side of the car. He leaned across the top of the car. "Yeah, we'll keep in touch. If you ever get the notion to visit our nation's capital, you have to look me up. Of course, I'd have a better chance of seeing a snowball in hell than ever coming to Boise, Idaho."

They both laughed.

Reggie sighed and shook his head. "Man, we had a hell of a time out here, didn't we, Mac?"

Mac didn't answer. He waved his hand, and Reggie picked up on the gesture.

"Yeah, you're right. I don't like long goodbyes either. See ya, Mac."

He got in, punched the car into drive, hit the accelerator hard, and screeched away, leaving a small patch of black rubber. He was headed back East.

CHAPTER 18

WASHINGTON, D.C.

The thermometer read 98.6 and confirmed what Tracey Marshall had suspected: She didn't have a fever. She sat up straight and braced her back against the pillow rest. She contemplated whether to take more cough syrup. She decided she'd wait a little longer because she wanted to finish the last two chapters in her Danielle Steele book before falling asleep. She pulled the bedspread up around her as Clayton walked out of the bathroom. She looked over and noticed that he looked handsome in his tuxedo. He leaned over and kissed her on the forehead.

"Honey, I'm sorry you don't feel well, and you know I'd stay home with you tonight . . . but I have to be at this fundraiser to represent the firm."

Tracey nodded her head and added, "Yeah, I know. I know. I'll be okay. So don't worry about me. I'll talk to you . . . " She hesitated. "Whenever."

He quickly moved away from her and said, "I'll check on Stockard on my way out."

She coughed, but she managed to say before he exited the bedroom, "She's fine. She's asleep. We'll be okay."

She heard his rapid footsteps down the stairs, the front door shut, and soon after the garage door opening and closing. He was gone. Off to another office function or . . . whatever.

She picked up her book from her bedside table. She removed the bookmarker and stared at the pages. She attempted to read, but she knew it was no use. That irritating feeling was gnawing at her again. The one that made her sick in the stomach. The one that always made her stop and think about her situation. More specifically, her marriage. She shut the book and went through her predicament, asking and thinking to herself, *Will things ever change?* Here she was in this gorgeous home by most people's standards. Married for three years to Clayton Worthington, an aspiring young attorney. Mother of a wonderful two-year-old daughter, Stockard, and pursuing her own career as a third-grade elementary school teacher in Washington, D.C. So what could be wrong? Just everything . . . everything. She put her head in her hands. For months now, she had been depressed, and it worried her to the extent that she sought relief through her doctor who prescribed antidepressants. It helped a little, but she really didn't feel better until she finally admitted to herself that she wasn't happy in her marriage. She also concluded that Clayton wasn't happy either, hence his seemingly always looking for an excuse not to be home. He was staying out later and later either at the office or just "out," according to him. If they ever did have a moment to be together or talk, it was always about him and his career, never hers.

She pulled a tissue from the box on the bedside table and sneezed before wiping her nose. *Probably picked this up from one of my little darlings at school,* she thought.

She pulled her knees up close to her body and stared at her bedroom walls.

The telephone rang interrupting her thoughts. She glanced at the alarm clock on the table. It was eight o'clock in the evening. She knew it could only be one person. She picked up. "Hi, Mom."

"Hello, Tracey. I just wanted to see how your cold was coming along."

"It's all right, Mom. I'm in bed reading."

She rolled her eyes and looked up at the ceiling. She wondered whether she had just lied to her mother, which she didn't like to do, especially now that her dad was gone. He had passed away a year ago. Although she and her mother were much closer now, she still realized that her mother was virtually all alone. She was a lonely woman for the most part and just needed to talk and stay close to her children. She supposed that tonight was her turn to keep her mother occupied. She also quickly rationalized that it was only half a lie. She would have been reading if she could have just settled down and concentrated.

After listening to her mother for over an hour telling her about all the things she planned to do to the house, her mother asked whether she, Clayton, and Stockard would like to come over for dinner the following Saturday. She normally would have said yes just to appease her mother, showed up with Stockard, and apologized for Clayton not being able to make it due to some work commitment. She labored over the invitation but decided to decline it. When, as expected, her mother asked why she wasn't coming, she concluded that she would tell her mother how she really felt and the reasons why her marriage was on the rocks. However, she didn't want to spend another hour on the phone going through the details this particular night. After a long pause, she told her that she would meet her for lunch the next day. Unfortunately, her mother insisted on a few more details, so she had to at least admit that she had a problem and would explain everything over lunch. Her mother reluctantly accepted the partial explanation and agreed to lunch the following day. She said goodbye, hung up the phone, continued to stare at her bedroom walls, and wondered what she was going to say to her mother.

CHAPTER 19

Tracey's mother sat with her mouth agape as she realized that the discussion with her daughter was nearly at an end. Tracey had opened up and explained her side of the story. She hoped she had answered all her mother's questions and responded to all her suggestions. They had talked about marriage counselors, which was out of the question because Clayton wouldn't bring himself to admit that they needed outside help in their marriage. It was another negative from him on getting their church minister involved. The barrage of questions was relentless. Her mother was from the old school of thought that dictated you stand by your man no matter what. Tracey had stood her ground in anticipation of her mother's disappointment and slight anger at her daughter's failing marriage. She felt she had handled her mother as well as could be expected, but after all, it was her life and her decision. The only real breakdown came when her mother asked about her grandbaby. They both became teary-eyed before she grabbed her mother's hand, explained once again, and hopefully convinced her that Stockard would be fine. Finally, her mother accepted her decision.

They sat quietly at their table. Neither spoke. Suddenly, her mother got up from the table.

"I'll be right back."

Tracey thought she was going to the restroom but was surprised as her mother exited the café. She became a little nervous but relaxed when she looked out the window of the café and saw her mother go out to her parked car and open the trunk. She looked puzzled as her mother reentered the café with a brown shopping bag.

Her mother sat back down, reached in the bag, pulled out an old shoebox, and handed it to Tracey. Still perplexed, Tracey took the shoebox.

Her mother's voice quivered. "I should have probably burned them. Lord knows your father and I had many an argument over them. I told him I threw them away, but for some reason, I couldn't. I kept them in the attic and lately in the car . . . just threw them in the trunk."

Tracey's eyes were questioning as she looked at her mother. She slowly lifted the top off the box. She gasped as she saw a bundle of unopened envelopes bound by a thick rubber band. She picked up the bundle and looked at the visible postmarks and return addresses . . . Vietnam. She dropped them back in the box and stared at them because she was in utter shock. "Oh, Mom, don't tell me . . ."

Her mother interrupted. "Honey, I'm so sorry, so very sorry. Your father and I only wanted what was best for you." She grabbed Tracey's hand and tearfully added, "I can't undo what's happened, but I've suspected for some time now that you and Clayton were having serious problems. I just hoped it would work itself out. And when we talked last night, I just sensed that something was terribly wrong, and I felt I had to at least give those to you. For whatever it's worth. Just to set the record straight."

She squeezed Tracey's hand. "And, yes, to clear my conscience. Forgive me, honey."

Tracey slowly removed her hand. Tears streaked down her cheeks. She picked up the letters again and flipped through them. *There has to be at least forty letters,* she thought. *He did write to me. He did. And I never believed him. I just blew him off.*

"Tracey, are you alright, honey?"

Tracey put the letters back in the box and put the lid back on. She wiped her face and answered her mother.

"It's okay, Mom. I'm alright. What's done is done." She sniffed. "Thanks for explaining, and thanks for giving them to me. I'll . . . well, I don't know what I'll do. I guess I'll eventually get the nerve to read them, but not right now."

Her mother handed her the shopping bag. Tracey placed the box in the bag before standing.

"Well, I guess that's about that . . . and about all I can handle in one afternoon." She went around the table, leaned over, and kissed her mother. "It's been a great lunch, Mom, but we'd better get going. I have to pick up Stockard at the babysitter's. I'll walk you out to your car."

CHAPTER 20

Reggie pulled the sun visor down and looked in the mirror to adjust his necktie. Satisfied that he had managed to tie an appropriate knot, he flipped the visor back up. The gas station attendant came up to the driver's side of the Mustang and said, "Nice wheels."

Reggie smiled, nodded, and replied, "Thanks. Fill her up."

As he sat at the two-pump gas station in the heart of Georgetown, he observed his surroundings. The city appeared to be coming alive as cars, trucks, and transit buses formed a steady stream of traffic all jockeying for position as they headed north on one of the busiest corridors in the city. He had been back in D.C. for three days, and his body clock was just getting acclimated to the bicoastal time difference.

California seemed like a long time ago already. The most vivid thing in his mind now was the long drive back to the East Coast. He remembered how he had decided on taking the southern route from San Francisco to Washington, D.C. It was a much longer route, but he didn't want to chance trying to get over the Rocky Mountains and all those humongous Midwest states like Montana and Wyoming. So he headed south down to Los Angeles and then cut across east to Arizona, New Mexico, and Texas, then headed north toward the East Coast. The entire trip had taken five days and nights. He had never seen the western and southeastern parts of the United States, so the trip was fascinating, scenic, and exciting, with one exception. He shrugged at the thought of what happened to him in Texas. But now that he was safe and sound in D.C., he had to really count his blessings that he had survived the trip. *Only in America,* he thought as he recalled that memorable night.

It was the third day of his trip, and he had been driving since sunup. He had crossed the Texas border and was headed east on Interstate 20 just at nightfall. He was tired but wanted to reach a motel in a small town west of Dallas before calling it a day. He was cruising along at about seventy miles an hour and listening to one of his tapes when he noticed headlights rapidly approaching his rear. Since he had been the only one on the two-lane highway in both directions for the past fifteen miles or so, he thought whoever it was would just pass him. He checked his speedometer and was satisfied that he was driving within the speed limit. If it were a cop, he wouldn't get pulled over for speeding. However, rather than passing him, the vehicle came right up on his rear bumper and bumped him.

"Shit."

He was startled and petrified as he temporarily lost control of his car and found himself straddling the centerline of the highway. Once he regained control and got back in his lane, he attempted to speed up, but the vehicle he had now determined was a pickup truck sped up also. He looked through his rearview mirror but could only determine that the truck behind him had two occupants. They flashed their bright beams, and the glare prevented him from seeing anything else. He thought about slowing down but decided it would be too risky since these were definitely idiots tailgating him. The only thing in his favor was that the highway was straight, and at the moment, he and the shitheads riding his bumper were the only vehicles on the road.

He pushed the accelerator on the Mustang down, and the 289 horse-power V8 engine responded. He was doing about ninety miles per hour and had separated himself from the truck. He relaxed a little, thinking the two occupants had decided they had enough of fun and games. It would have been great if he were right, but he wasn't. He looked out of his side mirror and saw the truck coming up on his left in the opposite lane. *Maybe they are just going to pass.* He let off the accelerator a little, and the Mustang eased back down to seventy-five miles per hour.

The pickup came up fast on the driver's side, and Reggie glanced over to see the occupants. His eyes caught the man on the passenger side leaning out the window with a beer bottle and brandishing a shiny pistol. Instinctively, he ducked his head and shouted, " *Aw fuck!"*

He definitely didn't want these guys in front of him. His next reaction was to hit the accelerator hard. The Mustang bolted back up to ninety miles and then a hundred miles an hour. It reached 110 miles per hour before he raised his head from its hunched position and could see more clearly. He quickly glanced out of his rearview mirror and could see the pickup truck some hundred yards back. He wasn't going to relax this time or allow the pickup to catch up with him. He held the accelerator down as the night countryside appeared to be a big blur. He saw building lights fast approaching ahead. *Must be the motel,* he thought. He could stop and get to a telephone to get help. He braked and slowed down as he wheeled into the motel/gas station a little faster than he would have liked. Dirt, gravel, and a cloud of dust catapulted from the ground as he abruptly halted the Mustang in front of the gas pumps. He rushed from the car and headed for the gas station's screened door. He looked back to see the pickup truck blow by. The truck passenger hurled a beer bottle, and it careened off the top of the Mustang and landed between the gas pumps spewing its contents. The bearded passenger leaning out of the window yelled out "hee-haw" as the pickup disappeared down the highway.

He was able to get to a telephone and call the police, but by the time they arrived an hour later, there was little they could or would do. As a matter of fact, he wasn't quite sure that the two officers that responded to his call even believed him. He showed them the dent in his rear bumper where the truck had bumped him. He pointed out the chip on the top of his car from the beer bottle. He even suggested that they take the bottle back to the station and dust it for fingerprints.

They looked at him, laughed, and said, "This ain't *Dragnet*." And later added, "Just take it easy, son. We'll check it out. Of course, it would help if you had a license plate number and a description of the vehicle or the occupants."

Reggie realized his precarious position and finally just dropped it. He checked into the motel, put a chair up against his door, and sat up on the bed fully clothed half the night before drifting off to sleep. He was extremely tired but left at sunrise the next morning. He just wanted to get the hell out of Texas.

"That will be ten dollars, sir."

Reggie reached in his wallet and handed the station attendant a ten-dollar bill. He adjusted his tie one more time and pulled out of the gas station and into the stream of cars headed north on Wisconsin Ave. He had managed to make two traffic lights before being snarled in stopped traffic at another light. He checked his watch and determined that he still should be able to make his appointment with no problem. He smiled as he thought about the next hour or two. Today was the big day. His face-to-face interview for his new job at the car company. Although the recruiter back in California had told him a little about the job, he still didn't know what to expect. He convinced himself that he was as prepared as he possibly could be. He had borrowed money from his mother to buy the suit, shirt, and tie from Sears. It was their cheapest line of menswear. He was hesitant at first to ask his mother, knowing that she was in no position to give him money. He knew it was tough on her just trying to keep a roof over the heads of the family. However, he believed deep down that this upcoming interview was a tremendous opportunity. He felt he had to look the part. So he borrowed the money with the rationalization that somehow, someway, he would pay her back and fulfill his dream of getting her and the family out of the projects.

The traffic light turned green, and he was able to get around a couple of cars making a left turn and move into a more fluid flow of traffic.

CHAPTER 21

Thirty minutes later, Reggie flicked his turn signal and pulled into the parking lot for the Field Office of Nation's Automotive Financial Corporation. He followed the signs that indicated the visitors' parking area, which was completely full. He found himself driving up and down long rows of what he assumed to be employee cars.

He eventually found a spot somewhere near the end of the lot. He got out, locked his car, tugged on his suit jacket, and pulled his trousers out of his butt. He got a firm grip on his new and mostly empty briefcase, a good-luck-on-your interview gift from his mother and family, and headed toward the ten-story building. He entered the lobby of the office building, checked the directory, and determined what floor he needed. He heard the ding of one of the four elevators and quickly entered with several other people who were waiting. He stepped off on the third floor and looked to his left. He saw the huge doubled glass doors with "Nation's Automotive Financial Corporation" in bold gold letters. He sucked in his stomach, took a deep breath, and said to himself, *Well, this is it.*

He walked through the doors and entered the lobby area of the expansive office. There appeared to be hundreds of employees scurrying to and from rows and rows of desks. The sound of voices, chatter, and the steady clicking of typewriters echoed throughout the office. Although he had never been at a newspaper office, the sight of so many people looking busy reminded him of what he thought a newsroom would look like.

"May I help you, sir?"

Reggie turned and walked over to the receptionist. She had a headset on and was at a switchboard connecting telephone calls.

"I'm here to see a Mr. . . . " He reached in his suit coat pocket and pulled out a slip of paper and glanced at it to make sure he had the name right. "A Mr. Watkins."

The receptionist smiled, punched a button on the switchboard, and spoke, "Would you please tell Mr. Watkins that a . . . I'm sorry, sir. Your name?"

"Reginald Saunders."

"A Mr. Saunders is here to see him. Oh, okay, and thanks, Martha."

She punched another button on the switchboard console, looked up at Reggie, and said, "Mr. Watkins is on a conference call, but his secretary says he shouldn't be much longer and asked that you wait."

Reggie nodded.

The receptionist continued, "You can make yourself comfortable and have a seat right over there."

She pointed to a small area across from the lobby that had a sofa, two chairs, and a table with lots of magazines on it. He walked over, sat down, relaxed a little, and thumbed through a *Sports Illustrated* magazine.

He hadn't been sitting for longer than five minutes when there was a loud banging of the double doors and the shatter of glass. Totally startled, he looked up from his magazine and witnessed four masked-gunmen carrying sawed-off shotguns. They burst through the doors, yelling, "This is a holdup!"

Two of the men rushed right by him and into the hundred or so now screaming employees. One of the two gunmen yelled, "Everybody on the floor, and you won't get hurt!"

A balding man who looked to be in his late sixties was slow to react, and one of the gunmen hit him in the back of the head with the butt of the shotgun. He went down like a limb from a tree. Blood spurted from his head. Most of the women were hysterical and still screaming. One of the two gunmen frantically pointed his shotgun at the frightened employees and yelled, "Shut the fuck up, and get on the floor!"

A third gunman rushed to Reggie's left and to the far side of the lobby area. He hopped over a counter to what Reggie realized was a cashier's window. He pushed a dark-haired, stocky, and stunned woman to the floor. He started to rummage through cash drawers, looking for money. He had a brown paper bag and was quickly stuffing bills in it. The fourth gunmen stood in front of the office surveying the situation. Some whimpering could still be heard. The telephones were ringing off the hooks but went unanswered. Everyone was now on the floor, except for Reggie. He didn't know quite what to do. It was obvious that the gunmen had not seen him when they hastily burst into the office. He didn't want to make any sudden movement now and spook them. He could see and tell by the way they were dressed and the sound of their voices that they were all young and nervous, except for the fourth gunmen who sounded older. The gunmen at the cashier's window seemed to panic and yelled to the fourth gunmen, who Reggie now realized was the leader.

"Moe, there ain't no real cash, man. Just chump change!" He quickly pulled the woman cashier from the floor, pointed the gun to her head, and screamed, "Where's the money, bitch?!"

Reggie turned his head back and stared straight ahead. Sweat formed on his brow. He waited for the bang. The other two gunmen were still guarding the employees lying on the floor. Moe motioned to the gunmen at the cashier's window. "Let her be, Tank. You sure there ain't no cash?"

"I'm telling you, man, there ain't shit here . . . Nothing!"

Moe appeared to contemplate their next move when he suddenly spun around and saw Reggie sitting on the sofa directly behind him. He pointed his shotgun at Reggie. Reggie could see out the corner of his eyes but continued to stare straight ahead. He didn't want to look his killer in the eyes. Not to mention he was scared to death. His entire life raced through his mind. He had survived a war in Vietnam only to come back home and be wasted by a bunch of young thugs. He lifted his head and looked up at the ceiling softly saying to himself. *I love you, Ma.*

Time seemed to freeze, and everything was in slow motion. He heard Moe say something, but for some reason, it wasn't audible. He continued to stare straight ahead.

"You hear me, motherfucker? I said who the fuck are you?"

Reggie slowly turned and finally looked at his would-be assassin. He figured he had lived a good life, albeit a short one. He could only see the darkness of Moe's eyes through the slits of his mask. The eyes of a cold-blooded killer. He held his breath as he looked at Moe's finger squeeze the trigger tighter. He contemplated whether this would be a good time to answer Moe. His thought was abruptly interrupted when Tank yelled out again. "Moe, we ain't got much time, man. What the fuck we gonna do?"

Moe's finger eased off the trigger, and his madman's stare left Reggie's profusely-sweating face. The shotgun barrel that was pointed at Reggie's head was now pointed at the floor. Moe turned back to his accomplices and shouted, "Let's get the fuck out of here!"

Reggie heard police sirens in the distance. Three of the gunmen raced past him and fled out the shattered glass doors. Moe was the last to leave. As he backed out, he looked over at Reggie who had begun to exhale but feared he was going to go into hyperventilation. Moe winked, nodded, and whispered,

"Take it easy, bro."

Reggie pulled out his handkerchief and wiped his face. The robbery seemed to last an eternity but was over in ten minutes. The office was now in pandemonium as the employees realized that the robbers had left and for the most part no one was harmed. Several people scurried over to the injured employee and attended to his head wound. Everyone else was on telephones. The police arrived about five minutes later and began interviewing the employees. Reggie had made up his mind that he had enough excitement for a lifetime. He hadn't realized that the automotive finance business could be lethal. *Hell,* he thought, *I felt safer in Vietnam.*

After the cops interviewed him and determined that he was not an accomplice in the robbery, he decided to leave. He was picking up his briefcase when an older gentleman in a three-piece suit approached him. He extended his hand. "Hi, I'm Charles Watkins. Are you Saunders?"

Reggie shook his hand and replied, "Yes, sir." He was about to add, "And I'm just leaving."

But Watkins, who still held his hand, quickly interjected, "And you're here to interview for the automotive representative job, right?"

Reggie was a little reluctant to respond.

Watkins continued, "Well, the interview is over. You've got the job, son."

Reggie was speechless as Watkins's words settled in his mind. He couldn't believe what he was hearing.

Watkins stepped back looked at Reggie and added, "You just witnessed and went through a major robbery, and you didn't flinch. You were cool, calm, and collected throughout the ordeal. We need young men like you. So the job is yours if you still want it."

He extended his hand again, and Reggie spontaneously grabbed and shook it. Watkins smiled and added, "Welcome to Nation's Automotive Financial Corporation, Saunders."

CHAPTER 22

Reggie shook the tow-truck driver's hand and gave him the keys to the Mustang. He stepped back onto the curb as the truck drove away with his car in tow. Old Betsy had died on him the night before. He considered himself lucky that he made it back to his apartment in Anacostia in Southeast D.C. He had just dropped off his date, Rona, who worked at his office. Normally, he would have stayed over at her place for the night, but it had been a busy week for him with several dates already under his belt from the previous four nights. To put it plain and simple, he was too tired. Plus, he realized that he had originally planned to go to breakfast with this fabulous fox that he had met at a party the previous week. He and his body were finding it increasingly difficult to keep up with all his dating obligations.

He had a dilemma. He would have to put his morning breakfast date on hold now because of his car problems. He knew it was the engine. It had been knocking for a few days and using a lot of oil. The tow-truck driver, while not a mechanic, confirmed that he too thought it might be the engine block. In which case, Reggie feared the worse: he'd have to think about buying a new car. Not that he couldn't afford it now, but the thought of getting rid of his Mustang deeply concerned him. The car had served him well, and now that his job had taken off, he was making a lot more money; things were really going well.

He walked back toward his apartment building and waved at old Mrs. Bartley, who was peering out her first-floor window. He surmised she saw what was probably a spectacle to her: his car being towed away. She probably thought it was being repossessed. She was a friendly woman, but Reggie knew she was a busybody and gossiper. There wasn't much that happened in the neighborhood that she didn't know about. So it was no telling how she would interpret or relate this incident to the next person she encountered. Not that Reggie cared that much. For the most part, he loved his apartment building and his neighbors, even old Mrs. Bartley. He had been living there over a year now, so he knew everyone and vice versa. The building itself was pretty old, but it was conveniently situated southeast and a few blocks from the Pennsylvania Avenue Bridge. Its location made it an easy commute back and forth to his job in Northwest D.C. Also, it was just a hop, skip, and jump from Georgetown, which was his preferred stomping ground. He found himself in Georgetown every Friday night that he didn't have a set date. He frequented all the dance spots and was a regular at all the singles bars. It seemed that he always scored with the women, especially when he used the "Silk" line. It was still solid gold.

He looked up at the three-story building before entering. On some nights he could come out of it and look south and actually see the Capitol from his side of the bridge. It was always a great sight, but it also made him realize the great divide from the haves and the have-nots. On the other side of the bridge, near the Capitol, were beautifully-renovated row houses that had attracted the young yuppies who worked for the government on Capitol Hill. It was hard to believe that just a few blocks away and over a bridge was the Anacostia section of Southeast Washington, D.C. with its many rundown buildings, lower-income community, and crime. He never let the crime and poverty bother him. He grew up in the city with its shortcomings. It was what he was accustomed to. The city was his home—his roots. It also gave him the drive and motivation that he had experienced when he was a kid helping his mother clean office buildings at night. He had seen the big offices, and the men walking around in suits, white shirts, and ties while carrying briefcases. They had fancy furniture in their offices and came to and left work in nice cars. He would sometimes stop his duties of emptying trash cans and take a moment to look around the big offices and the larger-than-large desks and the plush carpets on the floor.

He remembered the night that a man had walked in and caught him just standing in the office and gazing. He was actually rubbing his hands across the desk and chair. The man had startled him, and his first thought was that he was in big trouble. To his surprise though, the man said, "Say, young man, you like this desk, huh?"

Reggie had a lump in his throat and couldn't manage a response. He just looked at the man. Then the man said, "I think I have seen you in the building before. I guess you are helping someone out?"

Reggie swallowed hard and replied, "Yeah, my mom."

Even more surprising, the man put his hand on Reggie's shoulders and escorted him around the desk, swiveled the chair around, and said, "Sit down."

Reggie was spellbound but relaxed a little. He sensed that the man was actually being nice.

The man smiled and motioned. "See, things look a lot different when sitting on this side."

Reggie was smiling as he swiveled in the chair and softly ran his hands across the desk.

The man added as he pointed around the office, "Maybe one day you will be able to have an office like this." He shook his finger. "But you have to stay in school and work hard. It takes a lot of hard work."

He then motioned Reggie out of the chair.

Reggie smiled and said, "Thank you, sir."

Then he hustled over to the trash can, emptied it, and headed for the door. He never looked back, but he remembered what the man had said . . . "stay in school, and it takes a lot of hard work." He knew then that when he grew up, he wanted to be just like that man . . . a business-man working in a big office building and in a big office with a big desk. He knew it would happen one day. For now, he had to deal with trying to get another car.

He quickly reentered the building, jetted up the stairs, and opened the door to his second-floor apartment. He flicked on the light switch and went across the small living area to the wall where he had all his stereo equipment set up on shelves. He turned on his reel-to-reel tape deck and swayed to the smooth sounds of Wes Montgomery. He then flopped on his small couch and picked up the classified car section from the newspaper off of his coffee table.

CHAPTER 23

Reggie's feet were telling him it was about time to call it a day. He had been to five car dealerships and still no luck in finding a used car that he really liked. He was on "Auto Row" in Northeast Washington. It was a car buyer's paradise: nothing but used car dealerships one after another on each side of the street. He had no intention of walking to all the car lots, so he decided to go back to the dealership where his car had been towed. He thought maybe he could negotiate a higher price for Old Betsy in hopes of having more money to put down on a newer car. He had made up his mind that he was going to leave the dealership in something because it was getting dark and he didn't want to have to ride the bus back to Southeast. Plus, it was Saturday night. He needed some wheels!

He paced the lot again with the salesman. He was thinking about negotiating a price on a black Ford Mustang that he had seen earlier. He sort of liked the car, but as he had told the salesman earlier, the newer style of the car bothered him. In his opinion, the manufacturer had taken a good thing and just made it bad. Maybe it was just loyalty and the memories of Old Betsy, but he was still contemplating buying it.

As he was thinking, a car transporter loaded with cars pulled into the lot. He turned and spotted a shiny, red sports car on the second level. He asked the salesman, "What are those cars?"

"Oh, those are some cars we have been expecting from D.C. Police and the Feds. They have been confiscated from gangsters, pimps, numbers runners, drug dealers, and the like."

Reggie followed the transporter to the back lot and walked over to it. Turning to the salesman who anxiously followed him, he asked, "Are they for sale?"

"No, not usually, not now. You see, Mr. Saunders, we have to wait to see whether the original owners will get them back. Most of the time it's up to the courts, and it could take months to sort it all out. So we just drop them off here in the back of the dealership and wait."

Reggie shrugged as he eyed the sports car. He could now see that is was a Corvette. He climbed up on the car transporter to get a better look.

The salesman yelled up at him. "Hey, Mr. Saunders, you had better be careful! Our insurance won't cover you up there."

Reggie wasn't concerned. He was familiar with these types of trucks. He had driven similar ones when he was in the Air Force, particularly in Vietnam, where he had had to offload jeeps and other vehicles. He reached the car and leaned in to see the inside. It had light-gray leather seats, automatic transmission, smoked glass T-tops, AM-FM radio with tape, power windows and seats, air conditioning, and a mean set of Mag wheels. His eyes were like saucers. Perfect, just perfect!

He quickly climbed down and spoke to the salesman. "How much?"

"Uh, Mr. Saunders, like I said, these cars are not for sale . . . at least not yet."

He was truly disappointed but gave it another try. He patted the salesman on the shoulder, now noting for the first time "John Harriman" on his name tag, "Johnnie, my man, isn't there something we can do?"

He looked back at the Corvette. "That's me, Johnnie; that's me. I've got to have it. We've got to find a way to make this happen."

"Mr. Saunders, hey, I would like nothing more right now than to sell you that car, but like I . . . " He hesitated and said, "Wait a minute."

Harriman walked back over to the transporter and yelled up to the driver who was on the third level.

"Hey Joe, where's your inventory control sheet?"

A burly man, who was connecting the ramps to start the process of unloading the cars, looked down at the salesman and replied, "You don't think I'd carry them up here, do you? They are in the crew cab. What do you need?"

"Hey, thanks, Joe, no problem. I just want to take a quick look at where these cars are coming from."

Joe stopped what he was doing and climbed down to the second level and then to the first. Joe and the salesman could now talk without yelling.

Joe held on to a ramp guard and leaned across one of the cars on the lower level before continuing. "You don't need to look at the sheets. I know where I picked up all these cars. Which one you talking about?"

Harriman pointed up to the Corvette and said, "The Vette."

Joe looked up, turned around, and smiled, "Oh yeah, the Vette. I picked that beauty up at the FBI lot." Still smiling, he said, "You know, as in the Federal Bureau of Investigation."

They both laughed. Harriman slapped Reggie on the back while leading him away from the transporter.

"Mr. Saunders, today is your lucky day. I think we are in business. Follow me."

Two hours later and after signing what seemed to be one million documents and no doubt his life away, Reggie was handed the keys to his red Corvette. Harriman had explained that he was able to purchase the car because it had been confiscated in a drug and murder bust well over a year before. The original owner was convicted and sent to jail for life, therefore, by law, forfeiting any rights to the car. Somehow and somewhere in the process, the FBI had lost track of the car, and it wasn't until over a year later through an internal audit that they found it sitting in one of their lots. The sales manager of the dealership had to clear a few technical and legal hurdles, but it was all done with a few phone calls and the right documentation. Harriman was quick to point out that Reggie was lucky because had the car been confiscated by the D.C. Police instead of the FBI, he would have been "shit out of luck."

Reggie had inquired why the difference.

Harriman just shook his head and said, "You don't want to know."

Reggie knew a little about repossessed cars because that was one of the things he was learning to do while working for Nation's Automotive Financial Corporation. At the time, he was too excited to pursue the issue any further. All he knew was that he was thankful for three things: One, driving around in D.C., the city appeared much different when looking from the inside of a Corvette. Two, women just seemed to gravitate to the car. Three, Harriman had kept his promise in expediting the purchase documentation so that he could go down to the Department of Motor Vehicles and sign up for his personalized vanity license plates, which arrived exactly thirty days later. The tags read in big red letters: "SILK 9."

PART II

CHAPTER 24

DETROIT, MICHIGAN

"**A**re you coming to bed anytime soon?"

Laura Hartsdale sat up in bed and flicked the remote control to turn off the TV. She waited to hear her husband's response. Moments later, she heard the toilet flush, and soon afterward, her husband, Daniel Hartsdale, lethargically walked out of the bathroom and sat on the edge of their bed. She sensed the tension in her husband. She sat up and started to massage his shoulders. "Still worried about the board meeting tomorrow?"

Daniel Hartsdale relaxed his body as he welcomed the gentle hands of his wife on his shoulders. He closed his eyes and thought that the next day was truly going to be a major test for him. He was scheduled to speak before the Board of Nation's Automotive Financial Corporation. Normally, there would have been little to be concerned about because he had spoken to the board on several previous occasions. Although he considered himself relatively new as the executive vice president in charge of all corporate operations, his track record was pretty stellar. Over the past two years, operations had gone relatively smooth. Profits were up; corporate stock prices were rising. Under his leadership, the corporation was on target to meet its goal of expansion and acquisition. Things couldn't be better. Yet Hartsdale had reason to be concerned. He opened his eyes and turned to his wife of twenty-seven years.

"Yeah, just a little."

Laura Hartsdale looked at her husband, rubbed her hands through his now-graying hair, and said, "You'll do the right thing."

He stood up, stretched his slim, six-foot-one frame, and scratched his head. He rubbed his eyes and began to pace from one side of the spacious bedroom to the other. He paused at the side of the bed and looked at his wife.

"I don't know, Laura. I mean the stats, profits, stocks, etc. are a no-brainer. I'm just not sure whether this is the right time or venue. You know how they say that timing is everything."

Laura Hartsdale sat back in the bed, drew her legs up closer to her body, and continued to attentively listen to her husband.

"I mean, a part of me says maybe it's too big a project to tackle. Just leave it. Take care of my career and move on." He started to pace the bedroom again. "But another part of me, that other side..." He looked at his wife. "You know that wild side says enough is enough and somebody's got to put it out on the table."

She smiled at her husband. She knew all too well about that other side of him. That side of him that wasn't wild, at least not as far as she was concerned. But that aggressive, liberal, kind, and sensitive side that made her fall in love with him through their college days and marriage. That side that got them both in lots of trouble participating in student protests and sit-ins at the university president's office. But in contrast, that was also the side that organized the serving of hot food to the homeless in the community on holidays. He always exhibited love and kindness for his fellow man. She often wondered how he managed to do so well in the corporate environment with its cut-throat politics and dog-eat-dog mentality. Yet somehow, he had survived and had done quite well. Now he was only one or two promotions away from being the president of one of the world's largest corporations.

She looked up at him and felt this might be when she could add in her two cents. "Daniel, you've gone over this one hundred times. You've done the research, and you know the current situation. So whatever you decide, it will be okay, and I will support you."

She held her arms out and gestured him to come to bed. He went over to his wife, hugged and kissed her, and then got into bed.

CHAPTER 25

Christopher Roden wiped his glasses and adjusted his suit jacket as he waited impatiently outside his boss's office. He checked his watch and confirmed that he was still early for his scheduled meeting. He opened his briefcase and pulled out the report that he had spent the previous night and early morning preparing for his boss. He thumbed through the pages and assured himself that everything was in order and all the statistical data had been checked and double-checked for accuracy. He pulled out and scanned a sheet of paper that was his checklist. Satisfied, he placed everything back in the briefcase, sat back, and thought about the big day ahead. The day that could change his future and career. He wasn't too keen on the idea in the beginning, but after all the research, it was difficult to argue the statistical data with his boss. He realized that this was a hot subject, and one that could make him or break him. He also realized that he had been in the corporate world long enough to know whether he was either on one side of the topic or the other. There was not much in the way of middle ground; it all depended on what camp he was in. He smiled to himself as he realized that he was on the team that was now in control. So just maybe they could pull this thing off. Deep down, he knew it was the right thing to do no matter what the outcome, and he had decided long ago that he was going to remain loyal to his boss.

His boss and mentor had pulled him up through the ranks. He never forgot that fact … a fact in any major corporation. You had to be lucky enough to catch a rising star, and then you rode their coattails. The catch or trick was: one, if you caught the right star, and two, if you didn't, if you were smart enough to know when to let go of that coattail and hope that your career wasn't a bust. He relaxed as he thanked himself for number one. He straightened up in his chair, looked at his watch, and smiled as Daniel Hartsdale entered his office.

"Good morning, Chris."

"Good morning, Dan. Can I get you a cup of coffee before we get started?"

Hartsdale brushed by as he shook his head. He turned on the lights to his office. "No, let's start going over this. We don't have much time before the board meeting at ten." Hartsdale went around to his desk, threw his briefcase on his credenza, and turned to Roden. "Have you got everything?"

Roden sat in the chair directly in front of his boss, opened his briefcase, and gave Hartsdale the report.

"Everything is there, Dan, and I have the boardroom set up for all the visuals you will need. The slides are set up, and here is the remote." He handed Hartsdale a small black plastic device with several buttons. Hartsdale took it, examined it, and then placed it on his desk. He opened the file and began to peruse its contents. Roden sat back silently as Hartsdale flipped through the pages.

After a moment, he looked up at his friend. They had been together for a long time. He and Chris had started with the corporation after graduating from college. Chris had graduated from Boston College and Hartsdale from Princeton. They took different paths within the corporation: Chris in Human Resources and Hartsdale in Operations. Their paths crossed numerous times by way of corporate conferences and work projects, and they had both been enrolled in a special corporate MBA program. They became close when they were paired up on several study projects. The early competitiveness that they each possessed soon gave way to mutual respect. It seemed that whenever Chris was promoted in the Human Resources Department, Hartsdale was promoted on the Operations side. After ten years of respective marriages, friendship, and families later, Dan caught the eye of the company president, and his career took off. It was evident that he was destined to be a leader. But he never forgot Chris, and as he rose up through the company ranks, he always found a position for him on his team. Immediately after being promoted to executive vice president of Operations, he named Chris as his director of Human Resources. Chris was loyal, a person that he could trust and a good friend, but most importantly, he was the right man for the job.

Hartsdale nodded his head. "This looks good, Chris. Now all I have to do is sell it to the board."

Roden nodded but remained silent.

Hartsdale flipped a few more pages of the file and continued. He stopped at a page and looked up once again. "But you know this really bothers me." He pointed to a specific number. "We have over 100,000 employees in the U.S., right?"

"That's the correct number, Dan."

"And it indicates here that .09 percent are considered minorities. Chris, that's not even one percent! How can that be?"

Roden didn't respond. He and Hartsdale had been down this road before, and he knew he couldn't defend the seemingly negative fact. Hartsdale knew he wasn't going to get a response. Hartsdale got up from his chair and walked around to the front of his desk to face Roden.

"Tell me, Chris, how is the corporation going to meet the competition? How are we going to forge ahead when we don't have representation to reflect our customer base? Our customer base, remember? According to the statistics in the report and all corporate financial filings with the SEC, Wall Street, and Standard & Poors, our customer base is at least thirty-five percent minorities. It's a fact, Chris, that people of color do buy and finance cars and trucks. The vast majority make their car and truck payments, and that translates to record profits for the corporation."

He walked back around the desk to his chair and continued. "We are one of the largest corporations in the world..." He hesitated. "Yet we have less than one percent minorities in our workforce. Not to mention at any kind of managerial or executive level, which of course, you being the head of the Human Resources Department, know quite well that the number is zero."

Roden stirred in his chair before responding. "You are preaching to the choir, Dan. I'm on your side with this issue. But it takes time to make sweeping changes in a corporation this large. We have to first recognize the inequities, then get a game plan that will require extensive recruiting from major colleges. Then there's specific training and bringing them into the corporate culture, and then we have to hope for the best. It all takes time."

Hartsdale leaned forward. "We don't have that kind of time, Chris. We've got to do something now."

Roden looked at his boss and made no further comment.

Hartsdale tapped his fingers on his desk, still thinking. A moment passed. Suddenly, he reached into a drawer and pulled out two file folders. He tossed one file across his desk to Roden. "I've changed my mind. I'm tired of showing statistics and preaching this topic with the board." He pointed to the file folder in front of Roden. "This is what I'm going to introduce to the board this morning."

Roden read out loud the file name printed on the cover of his folder. "The Phoenix Program?"

Hartsdale replied, "Yes, the Phoenix Program." He elaborated further. "I can't take all the credit. I was exposed to a similar program at an executive conference that the corporation sent me to last year. Executives were there from the U.S. and around the world. You name the industry, and there was an executive representing it. In presentations and separate meetings, they really sold me on the idea that the next generation of successful corporations is going to be the ones with diversified workforces. Anyway, I've been working on this for several months. What I just gave you is a rough draft. I'm counting on you to put the final touch to it."

Roden had a look of amazement as he flipped through the pages of the file. After a moment, he looked up and swallowed before speaking. "Dan, you just can't wave a magic wand or put a fancy name on a cover file and think it's going to change an entire corporate culture overnight."

"Why not?"

"Well . . . Well, I don't know. . . . It's never been done before."

"That's my point, Chris. It's got to be done, and it's got to be done now . . . and by us. So are you in or out?" Hartsdale glanced at his watch. "Because in about three hours, I'm going to announce to the board that my director of Human Resources has everything under control and the program will be implemented ASAP."

Roden, still in shock from his boss's new revelation, flipped a few more pages of the file. He rubbed his brow and spoke, "Needs a little work."

Hartsdale smiled and said, "I never said it was perfect."

Roden nodded and said, "I'm in. When do we get started?"

"Right now."

Hartsdale got up from his chair, walked over to the door of his office, and shut it. He sat back down and picked up his file. He addressed Roden. "Turn to page thirty-four."

Roden found the page.

Hartsdale continued. "I have identified ten male minorities across the country and internationally in positions other than file clerks, stockroom personnel, mail clerks, etc. You will certainly have your work cut out for you."

Roden had an inclination to respond but decided not to. He continued to study the file. Hartsdale observed Roden's silence and knew he had him thinking.

"Chris, I know in its present form that it's not a lot to work with, but here's what I need. I need you to pull the complete ten personnel files that I identified to make sure I didn't miss anything, work up a detailed evaluation on each, and hopefully confirm that they will become the first candidates to be in the program."

Roden nodded and began to pick up his things to leave. Hartsdale held up his hand to stop him.

"Chris, I also need you back up here in my office within the hour with an outline. Just brief bullet points of the program that I can present to the board. It doesn't have to be detailed right now. The board does not need to know the candidates. I will just have to dazzle them with my footwork."

Roden smiled.

Hartsdale continued, "After the board meeting, I want you back in my office so that we can go over the ten personnel files together."

Roden took a deep breath as he was processing his boss's request. "Okay, I'll be back within the hour with the bullet points of the program for your presentation. Then I'll be waiting for you after the board meeting with the files and my candidates. Hopefully, all ten will receive confirmations for the . . . " He looked down at the file cover page. "The Phoenix Program."

CHAPTER 26

THE PHOENIX PROGRAM

66❝I**n summary, and as you can see, gentlemen, the corporation is about to enter a new phase of competition. We can't rest upon our past achievements. We must continue to forge ahead, meet the challenges, and remain the leader. Simply put, we must diversify our human resources to take on the U.S. and global challenges that are ahead, and we must step up our managerial ranks to reflect our customer base. I'm confident that the Phoenix Program, properly implemented, will keep us out front and ahead of our competition.❞

Daniel Hartsdale stepped back from the podium as the lights in the expansive boardroom came on. The giant screen behind him went blank and the bold white letters of "The Phoenix Program" disappeared. The sixteen all-white-male executives adjusted their eyes and began to stir in their chairs. After a moment, Hartsdale stepped up to the microphone. "Any questions, gentlemen?"

He took a deep breath as he scanned the executives. He felt that his presentation had gone well. Chris had done a good job with the outline of the program and putting it all together on the slides. The statistics couldn't be questioned. All he needed now was the "buy-in." Was the corporation ready to take the next step? He watched as his fellow executives nodded and leaned over to one another with soft whispers. Of course, he couldn't hear what many were whispering, but he still felt the general mood was in his favor. However, at the far end of the board table, he saw a hand raised. It was Matthew Brenner, the man that Hartsdale was promoted over. Because there was no love lost between the two, Hartsdale cursed himself inside for not anticipating some sort of disruption from Brenner. He acknowledged Brenner with a nod.

Brenner smiled as now everyone in the room looked at him. "Thanks, Dan." He cleared his throat and stated, "You say that we," he spread his arms out as if to incorporate all the seated executives, "have to embrace this new concept of diversity right now. While I won't argue the statistics with you, my question is: Why the urgency? Surely we have time to get this done. And this so-called The Phoenix Program—I haven't had time to fully digest it. Is this the program we need to begin to address this problem that you foresee? What's the rush?"

A few of the other executives began to stir again, and the whispers produced an unnerving murmur. Hartsdale felt he was losing a few of them. He was cognizant of the boardroom politics and how executives were known to split off into little groups. It was always "the who's in power" and "the who's not." He realized that he had to address Brenner and respond in a manner that would shut him down. He raised his hands to quiet the room and was about to speak when the chairman of the board and president of the corporation, Curtis Livingston, stepped in and said, "Gentlemen, I realize that this concept is new to most of us, but I personally feel that this is our future course, and we must give it a try. So unless there is someone among you who is absolutely sure that this will not work, we are going to move forward."

Livingston paused and glanced around the board table and was satisfied with no response from the group. He then continued, "However, I will add one caveat." He looked up to the podium at Hartsdale. "This will be a pilot program. We are going to try this shoe on first before buying it. As Dan mentioned, Chris Roden, our director of Human Resources, will be heading up the program, so we will check back with Dan and Chris for a full report at our next board meeting, and we will see where that takes us. Dan, thank you for your introduction and presentation on the program. Gentlemen, thank you for your time, and have a great day. This meeting is adjourned."

Hartsdale observed the board members as they gathered their briefcases and lined paper pads and began to disperse from the conference table. Most of the executives seemed to acknowledge what the chairman had just said. He was headed back to his vacated seat at the table to gather the remainder of his things. A couple of executives came up to him, shook his hand, and patted him on the shoulders. Hartsdale looked for the chairman because he wanted to thank him for the unsolicited support for the Phoenix Program, but Livingston had already left the table and the boardroom. However, he did notice Brenner at the far end of the table talking to another executive. Hartsdale had a strange feeling that he had not heard the last from Brenner. He felt he would definitely have to get the Phoenix Program up and running sooner rather than later. He quickly left the room and headed back to his office, where he hoped Chris Roden would be waiting for him for an update on the meeting and further instructions.

Matthew Brenner returned to his office. He brushed by his secretary and entered. As he threw the Phoenix Program file on his desk, he barked through the open door, "Get Parker up to my office right away!" He sat behind his desk and flipped through the pages of the file. He clinched his fist and his face reddened. He threw the file back down. *Bullshit, nothing but bullshit,* he thought.

Five minutes later, John Parker, his assistant to Marketing and Sales, tapped on his office door as he entered. As Parker approached his desk, Brenner tossed the file across it toward Parker. Parker quizzically looked at it. Brenner pointed. "Do you know anything about this?"

Parker looked at the title, "The Phoenix Program," picked up the file, and gingerly flipped through the first few pages. Then he shook his head and said, "No, sir."

"Well, you had better get to know about it real quick." Brenner continued, "Because this is apparently the new direction of the corporation, according to our illustrious executive vice president of Operations."

Parker could see that his boss was furious. He quickly replied, "I'll get on it right away, sir."

As Parker was leaving his office, Brenner said, pointing to the file in Parker's hand, "John, we can't allow that to happen."

CHAPTER 27

Daniel Hartsdale returned to his office, and Chris Roden was waiting for him. He motioned to Roden to follow him as he entered, shutting the door behind them. He took a deep breath as he sat in the sanctuary of his chair behind his desk.

Roden asked him, "How did it go?"

Hartsdale exhaled and replied, "Better than expected. I thought I had hit a snag when Matthew Brenner openly challenged me."

Roden hunkered down in his chair a little. He knew Brenner and what he was capable of.

Hartsdale continued, "But before I could respond, Livingston stepped in and informed the group that I had the green light to move forward."

Roden looked puzzled but remained silent.

"Yeah, I hadn't expected it, but it was surely welcomed because it avoided a collision course and possible showdown with Brenner. I guess Livingston bought me some time, which brings me to you. You know how this works. I'm out on that limb now, and there is no one else out there with me. If the Phoenix Program fails, I'm all but done. If it succeeds, Livingston will get the credit."

Roden nodded in acknowledgment.

"So the ball is in our court, and I'm passing it to you. I have a thousand and one things on my plate right now, so it's up to you to get this program up and moving. However, I want you to keep me in the loop by way of weekly reports. The first thing I want you to do is to contact those ten employees whom we identified and get them up here. To make this work, Chris, we need all ten, so 'no' is not an option. Use whatever resources you need; just get this done. If you encounter a problem, contact me on my private number. Any questions?"

Roden nodded and added, "Dan, this is huge. I'm working through the file and trying to fill in the gaps."

Hartsdale interrupted, "But we can do it."

Roden stood up and said, "Okay, I'm on it. I will talk to you later this week. And Dan, one other thing: I'm going to have to get someone else involved if we are going to pull this off."

Hartsdale gave Roden a piercing look. "Who?"

"Greg Morton."

"Can we depend on him?"

"Absolutely. He's my best man."

"Okay, then do it."

CHAPTER 28

NATION'S AUTOMOTIVE
FINANCIAL CORPORATION
FIELD OFFICE, WASHINGTON, D.C.

O ver a year had passed, and Reggie was beginning to feel comfortable in his new work environment. He was quickly picking up on the ins and outs of the automotive finance business. He was beginning to understand the internal office politics and had wisely decided to walk the middle of the road because he was the only black employee . . . well, the only black male employee. There were a couple of black women who worked as file clerks. Occasionally, at lunch break, he would meander over to their table and join them. They were both older women and married with families, so there was never a potential of anything romantic happening. That's the way he liked it, because he had decided that Nation's Automotive Financial Corporation was where he wanted to work for a long time. This was his dream come true. The opportunity of a lifetime to finally leave the hood behind and work for a major corporation. To one day become a manager or go even higher and reach the top. To enjoy the privileges and, of course, the money. Even more important to him was helping his mother and maybe getting her and the family out of the projects. He wanted to help his sister, Autumn, who was now thinking about college. To him, it was always about family. Although he always had high aspirations for himself, when it was all said and done, it was always about family. Family came first. He knew he had to work as hard as he could and take advantage of the opportunity to be successful in a major corporation.

He found himself always looking around at the vast office with over a hundred white employees and two blacks busily going about their jobs. He was forever looking at the manager's huge office at the rear of the massive room. A couple of times, when he was working late, he would walk back to the manager's office and peek through the door as the cleaning people were vacuuming the thick carpet, emptying the trash, or dusting. He had never seen such an expansive room with all the fancy furniture and plaques and pictures on the walls. Plus, there was a secretary. He thought that it was cool to have your own personal secretary. He often would watch her during the course of the day, shuffling in and out, bringing coffee in the mornings, and sometimes ordering lunch or takeout dinner if the manager decided to work late. Peering at the huge mahogany desk, he could feel the surge of power. He exhaled as he thought to himself, *One day . . . one day.*

However, being the only black male, he had also decided that he had to be careful. Everyone seemed friendly enough—that was to say, everyone always spoke and appeared polite. The women seemed more friendly. However, he sensed that the men felt threatened in some way and that he didn't belong there. That he was there to take their job or something. He also sensed a very competitive air within the office, but that he anticipated. He knew that he would have to work twice as hard and manage everything they threw at him to be successful.

·

As he toed the line, he quickly was able to navigate the office well enough to stay on the good side of most of the people who mattered. He figured that all he had to do was to keep his nose to the grindstone and learn everything he could about his job within the corporation. However, as good as he felt about his current status, he sensed early on that his direct supervisor, Jim Lattimore, did not care for him. At first, he couldn't understand why. His best guess was the fact that Lattimore was from the South, Alabama to be exact. He wasn't used to seeing black men in suits and ties and conversing in the King's English. He once questioned Reggie about his background, especially what college he graduated from. Reggie responded that he attended a community college in California and graduated with an associate's degree. Lattimore just got a noticeable smirk on his face, shook his head, and walked away.

He realized that with Lattimore's position, he was the guy that could make or break him. Lattimore was an expert at "subtle racism." He was very good at flying under the radar with his off-color remarks like "them colored boys can really play some baseball" when referring to the one or two black baseball players on the city's professional baseball team. Or like when he was passing through the lunch room and asked one of the two black women eating their lunch, "What you got there for lunch? Ain't chitterlings, is it?" Or when Reggie overheard him speaking to a couple of other supervisors, making a derogatory comment: "If they would get off their asses and work like the rest of us, they wouldn't need welfare." Reggie quickly realized that it was one of those things that he couldn't put his finger on or say anything, but as a black man, he knew it was there. Every day before going to work, he would remind himself that he had to somehow try to stay on that asshole's good side, if there were one. These interactions with Lattimore crystallized the realization that being black in a predominately-white corporation would present challenges and individual roadblocks for him.

So he made a concerted effort to really know the automotive finance business. As he was now seeing it, the business seemed simple enough. The customer buys a car from the car dealer and gets it financed. Then the customer has to make the payments on time to the finance company. If the customer is late making the payments, the finance company sends the customer a letter and then calls him or her. If the customer still does not make the car payment, the finance company sends a representative or collector to make an in-person house call. If the customer still does not pay, then the finance company sends out a repo man and repossesses the car. This process seemed quite easy to understand.

They started him out on the phones, making collection calls to past-due customers. He found that he was actually quite good at talking with customers. He would instinctively put on his telephone voice. Not surprisingly, from some of the responses and conversations that he had when speaking to these customers, he could sense that most thought he was white. That always worked to his advantage, as he would listen to their problems and come up with creative ways to keep them paying and staying in their cars. It gave him a great deal of satisfaction each morning when he arrived at work to see that the mail clerk had left a pile of envelopes with car payments on his desk, all addressed to his attention.

The part of the financing business process that he had not counted on was that when he was assigned house calls, which always seemed to be in the poor sections of D.C. and in almost always in the black neighborhoods, there was no repo company available. He was told in no uncertain terms on more than one occasion by Lattimore that he, Reggie, was the repo man, and he had better get used to it.

He stepped up to the challenge and accepted each house call assignment with a smile. He was very familiar with the black neighborhoods as well as the occasional white neighborhoods that he was sent out to collect car payments. It didn't matter what door he knocked on, he always presented himself in a professional manner. It started with the way he was dressed, always in a shirt, tie and business suit. Then he added the smile. That combination usually broke the ice and diminished the stares from both black and white customers that he was black. It never ceased to amaze him when the front doors opened and he would get the up and down look from customers. But once they saw the smile and heard his polite introduction, he would always notice the relaxed calm that ensued, which immediately set the tone and worked in his favor. After talking with and listening to the customer, he most often found a way to get the customer to pay something on their past due payments and stay in their cars. That part of his job made him feel like the insurance man who used to come around his neighborhood. Everyone loved the insurance man who was all dressed up in a suit and usually driving a big, fancy car like a Cadillac, collecting insurance payments from families that sometimes could not afford to pay. He remembered the insurance man telling his mom on many occasions, "I know the payment is one hundred dollars, but if you could just come up with a minimum payment of ten dollars, I can keep the policy current."

He enjoyed helping customers, or rather, families, to keep their cars because after their homes, he knew that their cars were the most important things to them. Generally, it was a status symbol to own a car. But in the hood, it was a necessity because no one wanted to have to depend on getting to work or anywhere else in the city on the D.C. bus.

While sometimes he would have to go the repossession route, in a majority of cases, he was able to get the customer to voluntarily give up the vehicle with hopes of maybe getting it back before the company sold it. He realized that he was becoming skilled at collections, especially on the streets of the predominantly-black neighborhoods. His coworkers were beginning to notice. He had established a reputation: if you wanted an assignment concluded, give it to Saunders. He loved what he was doing and felt that he was truly living the dream.

CHAPTER 29

Jim Lattimore snubbed his now unlit cigar in the ashtray on the corner of his desk. He leaned back in his chair and stared across the office at Reggie, who was talking to a customer on the telephone. Lattimore observed the big smile on Reggie's face. He had heard the buzz around the office from the employees who reported to him that Reggie was doing a fantastic job. He picked up his wrist strengthener and squeezed it repeatedly while clenching his teeth and thought to himself, *I didn't think that little son of a bitch would last this long. He doesn't belong here, and I'm getting tired of looking at that smiling face.*

He observed Reggie a little longer and then squeezed one last time on his wrist strengthener. He sat up in his chair, smiled, and thought to himself, *Well, what's a supervisor to do?*

Lattimore then yelled across the office, "Hey, Saunders, get over here!"

Reggie, along with several other coworkers, heard him. His fellow coworkers hunkered down because they all knew that when Lattimore yelled, nothing good was going to happen. Everyone was well aware that Lattimore ran the office, and people didn't make a move without consulting with him. He stood a little over six feet, and he relished intimidating employees. Plus, he always walked around with a stubbed-out cigar in his mouth for effect.

Reggie slowly got up from his chair and started walking across the massive office in the direction of Lattimore, observing heads bowing down to avoid eye contact as he passed each employee's desk. He wondered to himself, *What now?* Up until now, he thought he had done a good job of avoiding Lattimore. He kept his nose to the grindstone and just did his job.

As he stood in front of Lattimore's desk, he felt his heart pounding as if it were going to jump out of his chest, but he managed to control his breath and politely said, "Did you want to speak to me, sir?"

Lattimore looked up at Reggie, smiled, and threw a little black book across his desk. "Here, hotshot. Let's see what you are really made of."

Reggie picked up the book and flipped through the pages. There were only five pages. He noted that each page was a collection assignment of a customer that was past due . . . way past due.

Lattimore was enjoying the expression on Reggie's face. He added, "You've got until month's end to get these assignments cleared." Lattimore stood up and leveraged his height advantage. He leaned over and whispered into Reggie's ear, "You've got a company car so I don't want to see your little smiling face back in the office until it's done. Any questions?"

For a moment, Reggie was speechless and thought, *What the fuck? These are the five worst collection assignments in the office and in the worst neighborhoods.*

He had been working there long enough to know that none of the other collectors ever left the office to even try to collect from these customers in person. He stepped away from Lattimore with his heart still pounding and said, "I'll do my best, sir."

As Reggie turned and left, Lattimore said to himself, *The hell you will.*

CHAPTER 30

Two days had passed, and Reggie had had no luck in concluding the five past-due assignments. He still had two weeks until month's end, but time was running out. He sat frustrated in a booth in the miles-long sandwich shop in northeast D.C. As he ate a foot-long hotdog and sipped a Coke, he flipped the pages in the black book again as if something miraculous were going to jump out at him. He went through his mental process again. He had tried the telephone numbers. All were disconnected. He checked last-known addresses, and all had returned mail. To make sure he hadn't missed anything, he had driven by the last-known addresses several times at both day and night. He drove there as early as two, three, and four in the morning, and he still got nothing. The only option he had left was to start knocking on doors and hoping for a breakthrough.

He started by contacting relatives and friends that the past-due customers had listed on their credit applications. Most answered their doors but never gave up any information on the customer. No one seemed to know where anyone was. This, of course, was bull, but he had to go through the motions and thank them for their time and speaking with him. He had almost resigned himself to giving up and returning to the office to face Lattimore and an uncertain future when he thought of one last element that characterized the hood.

At some point in time, the guys—and these past-due accounts were all guys—would come to see their mothers. This was a fact. So he changed tactics. Instead of roaming the neighborhoods in the wee hours of the morning, he concentrated only on the mothers' last known addresses at varying hours during the day and late evenings. If he knew anything, he knew that dinner time was a definite lock.

After three days, it paid off.

He had spotted three of the cars. In each case, he enlisted the help of his sister, Autumn, who had just gotten her driver's license. Although like a majority of families in the hood, they had no car, for some unexplainable reason, it was a must to get a driver's license. He figured everyone had the dream that someday they would get a car. So Autumn was itching for an opportunity, any opportunity, to drive.

To his surprise, she followed his instructions precisely and never seemed to be fearful or acknowledge the possible danger. However, he made sure to never put Autumn in harm's way. He would pick up a company car from Nation's Auto garage and let her drive the company car with him as the passenger. They would scout the surrounding streets after he spotted the car. Then, as instructed, she would pull up beside the delinquent customer's car, and as they had rehearsed several times, stay long enough for him to jump out. He would then use his set of duplicate keys to get into the car, start the engine, and hopefully pull out before the customer knew what happened. Autumn's job was as soon as she heard Reggie start the car, she was to hit the accelerator and get the hell out of Dodge. She was cautioned not to look back and not to stop until she met him at a predetermined location that was usually two to three miles away. They would meet up, and she would follow him to the repo lot. He would then drive her back home and give her twenty-five dollars. Not a bad gig for a seventeen-year-old. This system had worked for three of the past-due customers. They never knew who repossessed their cars; it was just the repo man.

Several more days passed, and Reggie was down to his last two assignments. Somehow, by a stroke of luck he was informed by the office that the fourth customer had sent a money order through the mail for the five past-due payments. He surmised that his knocking on doors and contacting relatives and friends, "rattling the bushes" as he called it, might have spooked the customer that the repo man was getting close, thus the money order. There was still no address on file for him, but as far as Reggie was concerned, the customer was now current and off the list.

With only one more assignment to go, he was feeling a little more comfortable and actually was beginning to believe he just might pull off this challenge. He looked at the assignment. Alvin Johnson, five payments past due, last known address unknown. He shook his head, noting to himself that he had to retrace his steps.

He again started with relatives and friends. He studied the assignment and had to thank the car dealer on this one because Mr. Johnson had listed several relatives and friends beyond the one or two that was required to buy a car. He had spoken to two of the relatives on his first go around and struck out. He never got the time to finish up the last three because he got caught up in the process of repossessing the first three customers' cars. There was only so much he could do in the course of a couple of days. One of the remaining relatives on the list was a cousin.

To his surprise, there was an actual address. He thought to himself that with all this additional information, the boys in the office could have easily followed up to locate Mr. Johnson just by getting in a company car and personally contacting the listed friends and relatives. Maybe they could have located him or the car before the account became so far past due. Of course, he knew the reason why they didn't. They were afraid to work in the "bad" and black neighborhood.

He decided that he would see if the cousin's address was valid. Since it was in upper-northwest D.C., notably a pretty rough section of the city, he decided not to ask Autumn to ride with him. He knew she wouldn't be happy to learn about the missed opportunity to make another twenty-five bucks, but he had a gut feeling that it was safer to let her sit this one out.

The next day he went to the auto garage and jumped into a brand-new Chevy Malibu. It was teal green and only had fifty miles on it. It was the best part of the job—if you were assigned to go out on the streets, thanks to Lattimore, the company would let you use a company car for your troubles. Although it stuck out like a sore thumb as he surveyed the surrounding neighborhood, he was glad he didn't have to use his 'Vette. With the Malibu, he was hoping that the folks in the hood would think he was indeed the insurance man. His basic plan was to check out the cousin's address beforehand to see if he spotted the car. If the coast looked clear, he would go solo and park the company car a couple blocks away and then walk to the car and repossess it. He had learned on previous occasions that it was always a risky way to repo the car because you never knew what to expect as you walked solo a couple of blocks through these neighborhoods.

He remembered the time when he had been jumped by a group of thugs who took his wallet and watch and busted his lip before he even got to the delinquent customer's address. He had been so shaken by the experience that he had to abort his original intention. He was lucky he'd made it back to the company car that was parked a couple of blocks away. It was still intact, so he had gotten the hell out of that neighborhood. He never told the office about that incident.

To his surprise, on the first pass of the actual address, there sat Mr. Johnson's and Nation's Automotive Financial Corporation's Black 1979 Cadillac two-door Coupe Deville. The Cadillac was parallel parked tightly between two other cars. He had seen this type of tactic before. No way to get to the Caddy without damaging it and most likely the other two cars. He had to make a decision whether to keep driving by and hope for a better opportunity another day or night or stop and make contact. After considering the neighborhood, he contemplated the thought of a bad situation if he made contact, especially when he reminded himself of the time a customer brandished a knife when he knocked on the door.

He was beginning to think that maybe this job wasn't what it was advertised to be: "Wanted: Management Trainee." He was getting trained, all right—trained on how to dodge bullets. He remembered the time when he was shot at while rounding a corner after he had repossessed a car. None of these were pleasant experiences, and they were downright crazy when he thought about it. Somehow he managed to get through them. He had to admit to himself that he always felt exhilarated after he made it back to the repo yard with a car. *Definitely crazy,* he thought.

He made his decision. He slowed down and double-parked beside the Cadillac because there were no empty parking spaces on the narrow one-way street, and he wasn't about to park two blocks away and walk back through this neighborhood. No way. He got out of his car and walked up the steps to the row house turning around in all directions as he neared the door. He saw two men sitting in chairs on the porches on each side of Mr. Johnson's cousin's address. The two men briefly looked at him and then got out of their chairs and entered their respective houses. Before knocking on the door, he turned around and noticed a couple of people on the other side of the street sitting on their porch and watching him. He also noticed that another car had come up and parked in front of him, effectively blocking his exit if he by chance changed his mind and wanted to leave.

"Shit."

It was daylight and about one in the afternoon. He quickly weighed the odds and decided that the chances of him getting shot in broad daylight with witnesses were somewhat reduced, but in this neighborhood only slightly.

He drew a quick breath and knocked. Nothing. He waited another thirty seconds or so and knocked again.

He noticed a shade on the front window flutter as if someone had pulled it back to peek, but no one came to the door. Unless he could drive 100 miles an hour in reverse, leaving was not an option at this point since the other car still effectively blocked his car in. So he stood there and waited. Another minute passed, and the door finally opened.

He found himself staring up at a giant of a man. He had to easily be six-feet-six and weighed way north of 400 pounds. Reggie exhaled and introduced himself. "Good afternoon, sir. My name is Reginald Saunders, and I work for Nation's Automotive Financial Corporation. They sent me out to speak with a Mr. Alvin Johnson about the past due payments on the . . . " He turned around and pointed. "On the Cadillac."

The man who opened the door did not respond.

Reggie was about to add the obvious, "Are you Mr. Johnson?"

But before he asked, someone in the background yelled out, "Hey, Big Al. Who's at the door?"

The giant stared at Reggie and then spoke. "I'm telling you right now; ain't nobody taking my car."

Reggie raised his hands and said, "Oh no, Mr. Johnson. The company would never think of taking your car. That's why they sent me out . . . to, uh, talk to you." Reggie paused a second to gauge Big Al's mental state. He didn't want to push the issue and run the risk of a violent response.

"Uh, Mr. Johnson, I saw that you are a man that takes good care of your car. It's in immaculate shape, and I love those Mag wheels. They really set it off. Really cool."

Big Al shifted but didn't say anything. Reggie decided to go for the whole ball of wax.

"If I could just step in, I'm sure I can work something out with you on those five past-due payments to avoid any future problems because, like I said, the last thing Nation's Automotive Financial Corporation wants to do is take your car."

Big Al looked over Reggie's head and out at his car. He then stepped aside and motioned for Reggie to step in.

The shade to the front window was still closed as Reggie stepped into the semi-dark small room. The other guy who yelled out earlier, who he suspected was the cousin, was sitting in a chair on the opposite side of the room. There was a worn sofa and a scratched-up coffee table centered and facing a TV.

The cousin stood up and said, "Who da fuck is this dude?"

Big Al motioned him to sit back down and said, "I'll do the talking . . . Turn on the lights."

The cousin sat back down and flipped a switch on the wall just above his head. He slumped in the chair and then turned his attention back to watching the TV. As he sat, Big Al pointed for Reggie to sit on the sofa. He looked at Reggie. "So what you gonna do for me?"

Reggie pulled a couple of papers from his jacket pocket and replied, "If I can have a moment to explain and get you to sign these papers, we can get you current."

Big Al sat back smiling, showing at least three gold teeth.

Approximately thirty minutes later, Reggie got up and shook Big Al's hand and told him he was now current and good to go.

Big Al was definitely a little more relaxed, but said while pointing at the papers, "What about the 100 dollars you said I needed to do this? I told you I ain't got no money right now."

Reggie put up a reassuring hand and said, "Don't worry about it. You still have three more years of payments left, so I will make sure the company puts the 100 dollars at the end of the contract because we both know you will be better off three years from now, right?"

Big Al nodded. "You got that right."

Feeling that he was almost home, Reggie started to the front door and stepped out on the porch with Big Al. He saw that his car was still blocked in, and there were two guys standing beside it. He looked over at Big Al who nodded to the two guys. He walked down the steps toward his car. The two guys stared but moved away. They got into the car that was blocking him and pulled away. His knees were still shaking and his heart pounding, but he managed to get into his car, waved at Big Al, and drove away. When he got about five blocks away, he pulled over, exhaled, slapped his steering wheel several times and screamed, "Yes!"

As elated as he was, he had to calm down and halt his exuberance. He pulled back on to the street.

He had to seriously think how he was going to come up with the 100 dollars that Big Al didn't pay. He had thought about it at the time he was explaining it to Big Al, but he had been so scared when Big Al told him that he didn't have 100 dollars, he just went with it to get out of the house unharmed. He thought about it a little more as he was driving and came up with the only solution: pay it himself. However, the problem was he didn't have the money either. Payday was still several days away. He hated to think about it, but there was only one thing to do. He decided he had to make another stop before going back to the office.

CHAPTER 31

At approximately four in the afternoon, Reggie was pulling into the Nation's parking lot. He had a spring in his step as he crossed the lobby of the building and entered the elevator heading up to the third floor for the office. He had a grin from ear to ear as he pushed the office's big glass doors and went right up to the cashier's window and pushed the cash and receipt he had collected across the counter to a cashier. He then pushed through the swinging doors to the main office and strutted to his abandoned desk. He pulled back his chair and threw the now-empty black book across his desk hard enough so that all his surrounding coworkers would take notice. It didn't take long before the entire office knew that Reggie had somehow gotten the worst five accounts in the office either current or repossessed.

He felt like a rock star as his fellow coworkers came up to congratulate him. Even the manager, Mr. Watkins, came out of his office because of the heightened chatter. He looked at Reggie and shook his hand, saying, "That was quite an accomplishment, young man. You saved the company a lot of money because we were about to just charge those accounts off and take the loss."

Reggie continued to smile and said, "Thank you," all the while thinking to himself that he would have never pulled it all off if it wasn't for the last-minute cash infusion that he was able to secure after he made the stop to the projects where his mother and family lived.

His father wasn't living at the house anymore. Just one of the many times that his mother had kicked him out. So there was no extra money coming in. He had hated to ask his mother for the money because she was still struggling just to keep food on the table for his sisters and brother. But he felt he had no choice, plus he knew that he would be able to get it back to her with a little extra as soon as he got paid. When he explained to her why he needed the money, she told him she didn't have it but not to worry, that she would get it.

When she was leaving the house, Reggie realized what she was going to do: go next door to Mrs. Blanche's and borrow it from her. Reggie pleaded with her not to do that, deciding that he would just have to figure out something else, but she waved him off and said, "I know Blanche got the money 'cause she just hit the numbers. Plus, we both will have some extra cash this weekend when we do the Friday Night Specials."

Reggie knew right away what that meant. On Friday night, half the neighborhood would be over at his mother's house buying fried chicken dinners for five dollars. When his mother added collard greens, potato salad, and cornbread to the fried chicken, it became the best Friday night meal in the hood, and people lined up at the door. And if things really got going, there would be the craps game in the back room where his mother and Mrs. Blanche would take a portion of the winnings as house money. In other words, Mrs. Blanche and his mother would pocket the cash. After his mother came back with the cash, Reggie didn't feel as guilty for asking for the 100 dollars because he knew his mother's anticipation of income in a couple of days was right on.

He was still enjoying the office accolades as he settled in at his desk. However, he did make a mental observation that Lattimore was still over at his desk and had not come over to him. Actually, that was a good thing as far as he was concerned. Although he had concluded the five assignments and could relax a little, the less he saw of Lattimore the better. He thought about walking over to his desk and throwing—well, maybe handing—back the empty black book but thought better of it. Better to let well enough alone and for the moment enjoy his new stardom.

Things quieted down as the working day was ending. Some employees were beginning to start packing it in and preparing to leave the office. Before calling it a day, Reggie decided to go back to the stock room to pick up some office supplies to restock his working area on his desk. He had just loaded a box of staples, paperclips, pens, and pencils from an upper shelf in the stockroom when he heard the stockroom door shut. He thought nothing of it until he detected the strong smell of a cigar. He turned quickly and saw his worst nightmare: Lattimore coming toward him. There was nowhere to go or hide so he braced himself and acknowledged Lattimore's sudden appearance. "Uh, hello, Mr. . . . "

Before Reggie could finish his greeting, Lattimore shoved him up against the shelves, splattering the pencils, clips, and pens on the floor. This caught Reggie totally by surprise, and he was defenseless. Lattimore was breathing that nasty cigar breath in Reggie's face. He pulled Reggie closer, using his weight and height advantage, and said, "I don't know care who you are, where you came from, how you got that fancy sports car, or how you got those past due assignments concluded, but you're one lucky son-of-a-bitch that Watkins likes you. So, I'm going to say this just once: I'll be watching you from now on. And there're three things you had better not do."

Reggie could do nothing but look into Lattimore's bloodshot eyes and think that this man was crazy.

Lattimore tightened his grip. "Don't fuck with me. Don't fuck with the cash. And don't fuck with the gash." Then he lessened the pressure and stepped back from Reggie. He kicked the pencils, clips, and pens, opened the door, looked back at Reggie, and walked out of the stock room.

Reggie relaxed a little and tried to catch his breath. He became angry with himself for not standing up to Lattimore. But after he calmed down a little, he realized that doing nothing might have been the best choice. He rationalized that if there was any kind of altercation, he would be blamed for it and would no doubt be fired, because who would believe him over Lattimore? As much as his manhood was threatened, he had to just let it go, not mention the incident to anyone, and live for another day in the white man's world.

CHAPTER 32

Several weeks had gone by, and things were quieting down on the job. Reggie was feeling even more comfortable with his daily responsibilities. Remembering his encounter with Lattimore, he had managed to stay out of his way for the most part. "Don't fuck with Lattimore" was instilled in his mind as he fought with himself and questioned how long he could keep the charade going before something blew up. He didn't have any problem with not messing with the cash. That was never in his makeup, and he knew that he would be fired with no questions asked. The gash part, though, was proving to be somewhat problematic for him. He had to force himself to back off and sometimes out of the office social environment. He was still held in high regard by his fellow coworkers for his reliability in the job that he was doing. Now he was dressing the part even more with stylish suits and ties; he drove a Corvette. He was single, and he considered himself fairly good-looking. He had noticed that the single women in the office had become a little friendlier toward him. The smiles were flourishing. It was California all over again. He wasn't sure how he would handle the new attention, but he felt he should be careful because of Lattimore's warning and the feeling that he was being watched.

He had been invited out several times for after-work gatherings at the local bars. He had attended a few and had also gone to a couple of house parties. He couldn't explain it--maybe it was just plain stupidity, but somehow, without fail, Lattimore's warning would escape his memory, and he would succumb to his weakness: women. He would find himself, at a minimum, with his tongue thrust down a coworker's throat. One of those coworkers' throats belonged to Lattimore's niece. She was interning on her college summer break, and he was secretly seeing her. It had to be stupidity. There was no other explanation, except maybe it was his way of getting back at Lattimore, sort of an "In your face, dude."

But she was just one of the many women he was attempting to balance within his social life.

Outside of work, and more often than not, the "Silk" line would work when he was talking to women. However, what was even more amazing was when the women he would be talking to finally saw his Corvette and noticed the "9" on his license plates. They would invariably ask what the "9" was for. That would always lead into a sexy discussion with Reggie conjuring up an explanation. He would always say that he was the master of an ancient art. Of course, that would puzzle most women. At that point, he would have their attention. Then he would follow up by saying to them, "Repeat 'Silk 9' over and over again as fast as you can . . . and then faster and faster."

If he was at a bar and the young lady had drunk enough, she would become tongue-tied and "six-nine" would eventually register. Then he would ask, "Now, what do you hear yourself saying?"

Most women would smile and get the message, which usually became a prelude to the mood for the evening.

His story would be a little different if he was talking to men. If he was at a bar for drinks and someone asked about the "9" on his license plates, he would usually wink and say he had had a bet once that he could go to bed with a certain number of women in a forty-eight-hour period. The men would usually be confused, and ultimately someone would say, "So?"

Reggie would not respond for a moment or two, take a swallow from his beer, and then say, "I lost." He would pause another moment for effect and then say, "The bet was ten."

Of course, the men would just laugh and say, "No way."

Reggie would just take another sip of his beer, smile, and say, "You asked."

He had just moved to another small apartment in a better part of southeast D.C. that was even closer to the Anacostia River and a stone's throw from the "other side." He continued to dream up excuses of how to get women out of his bed and out of the apartment so that he could have some free time for himself. When he did have free time, he would think about the fact that he was living the dream and becoming a legend of sorts, even if only in his mind. However, he realized that he had to slow his nightlife down and continue to learn everything he could about the automotive finance business. He already felt he could do the job of some of the supervisors who were instructing him and directing him in written correspondence, collections, repossessions and customer service. He kept pounding it in his head that he had to stay focused on the big picture: becoming Mr. Reginald Saunders, Field Office Branch Manager in Nation's Automotive Financial Corporation.

CHAPTER 33

Days turned to weeks, and weeks turned into months. The day-to-day office business of receiving letters from customers, doing adjustments on customer accounts, making collection telephone calls, and, more often than Reggie liked, going out to repossess past-due customer cars became routine.

He had just returned to the office from the field and was sitting at his desk when his phone rang. Usually, when he received a phone call that quickly, it was from the customer whose car he had just repossessed. It never ceased to amaze him how those customers miraculously came out of the woodwork because prior to that the company didn't know where they were. That was to say, no address, no phone numbers, returned mail, etc. Only by very good detective work from the dedicated employees of the company, in this case, Reggie, would a lead develop to locate the car. It amazed him that the customer was all of a sudden alive and well and wanted to know what they needed to do to get their car back. They would be in the office usually within the same day of car repossession with the past-due payments.

He picked up the phone. It was Martha, Mr. Watkins' secretary. Mr. Watkins wanted to see him . . . right now. He slowly put the phone down. All kinds of thoughts raced through his mind, none of them good. Had

Watkins found out that he was sleeping with Lattimore's niece? That little voice in his head was saying, *Yeah, you, dumb shit. What were you thinking? Lattimore's niece? Man, are you crazy or what? He's going to kill you if he finds out.* He pounded his hand on his desk and silently said, *Shit, shit, shit. I should have just done the one and done thing . . . But no . . . Why? Well, maybe the getting back at Lattimore was driving me, but the real reason was that she was a freak in one respect and absolutely insane in another.*

He thought back when they were last together: that late evening and warm summer night. They had just engaged in an indescribable romp in bed. Afterward, to recharge, he had stepped out onto the balcony of her high-rise apartment, which overlooked a wooded park. Nothing but total darkness. He had only a bathrobe on. He had decided to recline in one of her chaise lounge chairs. She had called out to him that she was fixing him a drink. She came out on the balcony in a slightly-parted black bathrobe. She was holding a snifter of cognac and a lit cigar. She took a sip of the cognac and handed it to Reggie. She took a puff from the cigar and also handed it to him. She smiled and said, "Relax . . . relax."

The sweet taste of the cigar and the smooth burn from the cognac definitely relaxed him. He thought to himself as he looked out over the woods and darkness. *Man, it doesn't get much better than this.* Or so he thought. He looked down and could see and feel his bathrobe being parted. He gently laid the cognac and cigar down on the small table beside him. He couldn't believe but definitely felt what was happening. He slowly exhaled . . . Moments later, he entered seventh heaven! And that was that. It was foolish when he thought of the consequences if he was ever caught, but . . .

He shook his head to clear his mind of the memory. He pounded his fist once more, got up slowly, and headed back to Mr. Watkins's office. A few employees looked up as he passed, but no one seemed particularly interested in what direction he was headed. He passed Lattimore's desk and noticed he wasn't there . . . only ashes from a cigar in an ashtray.

Martha greeted him as he approached Mr. Watkins's office. Watkins's door was shut, so he stood in front of her desk. She motioned for him to sit down as she buzzed Watkins. She looked over at him nervously sitting and said, "He'll be with you in a moment."

Five minutes later her phone buzzed. She picked it up, listened, put the phone back down, and said, "Mr. Watkins will see you now."

Reggie took a deep breath and said to himself, *Whatever happens, keep your cool.*

He walked slowly into Watkins's office and immediately saw Lattimore sitting on a sofa to the right of Watkins. Lattimore stared straight at him but didn't speak. Reggie thought to himself, *Shit, I'm doomed.* Watkins motioned to Reggie to sit in one of the chairs facing his desk. Then he nodded to Lattimore. Lattimore got up, still not speaking, passed Reggie, and left the office.

Watkins rose from his desk and came around to face Reggie. He was of medium height and build with slightly graying hair and a receding hairline. In the months that Reggie had worked there, he had never seen Watkins much. He was the big boss, and for the most part, employees stayed away from him and his office. Watkins extended his hand and shook Reggie's. His grip was firm as he said, "Good morning, Saunders."

As Watkins was going back to his desk, Reggie took a quick moment to look around the huge office. Although he had peeked in and seen it before when no one was around, sitting there now, it projected a new and powerful presence with Watkins now standing behind his high-back upholstered chair. Reggie tried to clear his throat while he waited for Watkins to say something. He hoped that Lattimore wasn't coming back.

Watkins looked at him and then glanced down at a file on his otherwise empty desk. Reggie noticed the file with a pair of glasses sitting on top. Watkins sat down, picked up his glasses, and opened the file. He flipped a few pages. Reggie waited. Watkins closed the file and leaned forward.

"Saunders, let me get right to the point. You probably know that I don't get too involved with individual office personnel. I generally leave that to my office supervisors."

Reggie somehow nodded.

Watkins continued, "Every now and then, an employee file makes it to my desk, and I have to get involved."

Reggie stirred in the chair. His butt was sweating through his underwear, and it felt like it was glued to his seat. His mind was tripping, and he could think of a hundred things within the social circle of the office that he could probably get nailed on, all involving women, particularly Lattimore's niece. Dumb shit. But then again he thought, *Why would Watkins get involved unless some woman had blown the whistle on me? Dumb shit!* It was good while it lasted. He figured it was all over now. He snapped back to the present, and he was hearing Watkins for the first time.

"Anyway, Saunders, your file reflects that you have been doing a good job. You've managed to absorb what we have taught you, and from what I see and hear, you get along with your coworkers. So I suppose you are wondering why I've asked you here."

Reggie still couldn't believe what he had just heard but managed to utter, "Well, I'm not sure, sir. . . I—"

Watkins interjected, "I guess you wouldn't, young man. Well, either someone above is watching over you, or maybe you are just in the right place at the right time. In any event, the long and short of all this is you have been requested to transfer to Detroit."

Reggie's eyes widened in amazement, and he almost threw up. "You mean Detroit as in . . ."

"Yes, son, corporate headquarters."

Reggie slid back in his chair. "Uh, when is this supposed to happen, sir?"

"As soon as possible. Next week or the week after."

Reggie was extremely excited but paused as he remembered something. "Sir, I just signed a one-year lease with a full security deposit on my apartment. I can't afford to pay the twelve payments and . . ."

"Don't worry. All that will be taken care of by the corporation. You won't lose anything nor will you be on the hook for the lease. The corporation will provide you with a moving expense and assist you in finding a place to live. They will even subsidize your rent while you are in Detroit."

Reggie still couldn't believe what he was hearing, but he thought to himself, *Hot damn!*

Watkins got up from his chair and walked around his desk. He sat on the edge in front of Reggie.

"Saunders, I have to be honest. I don't know what this is all about, but apparently you have been chosen.

All you have to do is say yes, and everything else will be explained to you when you get to Detroit. The only thing that I can add is that you will be there for two years."

Reggie thought about the two years. Then shrugged his shoulders and said to himself, *Shit, after Vietnam, I could do two years anywhere.*

Watkins stood and extended his hand. Reggie shook it while nodding.

"Good decision, son. I'm sure you will do well. Just see Martha on your way out. She has all the paperwork and will coordinate everything with you. Congratulations and good luck."

Watkins went back to his desk and patted himself on the back. Although he had only two years left before his retirement, he didn't need any more blips on his record. Earlier, he had gotten the phone call from Detroit from a guy he didn't know personally. It was the director of Human Resources, Chris Roden. Watkins wanted to ask questions and get a better explanation, but he got the message loud and clear from this Roden fellow that Detroit wanted Saunders right away, so he needed to get the process moving. Watkins did as he was told. End of story.

After Reggie left his office, Watkins made a few phone calls to his cronies. The word was that the corporation was shifting toward some sort of Affirmative Action program. He wondered what the corporation thinking was and who was behind all this. Not that he had anything against Affirmative Action; of course, it had never affected him. Besides, no matter what course the corporation took now, he was bulletproof. In two years, he would be retiring. So the "Saunderses" of the corporation could do whatever . . It wouldn't affect him. He had done his part. Saunders was on his way to Detroit. He smirked to himself.

"Son, you are undoubtedly in for a rude awakening."

CHAPTER 34

It was Friday afternoon and almost quitting time. A few people had already left early. Several days had passed since his meeting with Watkins. Reggie relaxed while sitting at his desk, shuffling papers, and thinking about the reality that he was actually leaving. As far as office work was concerned, he was on autopilot. Many of his fellow coworkers had congratulated him and seemed genuine in wishing him well. From all the talk about corporate headquarters and Detroit, he had surmised that he was truly fortunate to get the opportunity.

Detroit was like some sacred or holy land. Only the gods, not mere mortals, lived and worked there. In some respect, he wondered whether he would be up for the task. It seemed that while everyone knew about headquarters, no one had ever been there, so no one could really tell him what to expect. Headquarters was a place from whence rules and regulations emanated. No one knew how. Whenever there was a phone call or memorandum from headquarters, everyone just jumped and went into hyper mode. Every now and then, an executive would come through D.C. and might visit the field office. Reggie would observe Watkins break out in a cold sweat, and the office would immediately go into that same frantic state.

He sat back in his chair and stared at the ceiling. It had been tough to hold back his excitement, but he knew he had to because he had learned that you never wanted to burn any bridges. It took a little time, but with the exception of Lattimore, the people in the office had been good to him. Some had even embraced him more than they had to. Not to mention the five to six women whom he was now dating simultaneously. It had been hectic trying to keep it all together with them not knowing about each other, plus staying out of Lattimore's way. On one hand, he thought to himself, only someone crazy would be doing what he was doing and actually enjoy it. On the other hand, he felt a little relieved because with him being transferred, the Lattimore situation would, at last, be over. He wouldn't have to deal with him ever again. He would miss Lattimore's niece . . . Man, would he ever, but a man had to do what a man had to do. As for the rest of the women he was seeing, he had already planned his exit—his long goodbyes to each. The dates, the days, the nights, the romantic rides in the Vette. Then *poof,* he would be gone.

Everything was pretty well set. His work was done. His apartment was taken care of just as Watkins had told him. He had money to cover moving and then some. He was like a lame duck just waiting for the last few days to pass and then the long drive to Detroit.

He interrupted his thoughts and looked at his watch. He snapped his fingers, reminding himself that he had to leave because he had to pick up beer, wine, and liquor to take over to his mother's house. His family wanted to get together and throw him a going away party. He had pleaded with his mother not to go through the expense because she really couldn't afford it, but he knew she was very proud of him. This would be her way of showing half the neighborhood her eldest child, Reginald Saunders, was now Mr. Corporate America. She had told him not to worry because she could always count on Mrs. Blanche and a few of her girlfriends to go in on some of the food. And as she said, "They were going to party."

He smiled a little as he thought, *Yeah, Mr. Corporate America.*

It had a certain ring to it. The smile was short-lived, however, because he knew the reality. He wasn't done yet. Sure, he had a good job now, drove a Corvette, and had lots of clothes and his own apartment in southeast D.C., but the truth was that he was only one step removed from the hood, the northeast projects of D.C., in the hood where he had grown up as the oldest of seven kids. The hood where his mother and siblings still lived. The hood where he decided as a young boy that he would somehow get out and never return. The hood where as a kid he was beaten up more than once because he wouldn't join a gang. Instead, he had to fake being "bad" and do things like steal candy from the corner grocery store to prove he wasn't soft or a sissy.

As he got older, the "bad deeds" escalated in severity. He would go across town with his running buddies and break into white folks' homes and steal expensive stuff like watches and jewelry. He remembered quite vividly when one of his buddies stole a car, and against his better judgment, he went along with it and found himself in the backseat with a couple of police cars in hot pursuit. Eventually, after speeding recklessly through the streets of D.C., they were caught. That episode had finally put the fear of God in him, even more so than the fear of getting beaten up by the project's hoodlums.

The only thing that kept him out of jail was that he had only been fourteen and was considered a juvenile. The driver and the other two guys weren't so lucky. He remembered the courtroom and the judge leaning over his podium before slamming his gavel down and saying, "Young man, after looking at your school record and listening to your probation counselor, I see that you are a straight-A student and you have never missed a day of school in three years. She also gave me a copy of your library card for the record."

The judge had quickly scanned the file in front of him. "It appears you spend a lot of time in the library and checking out books when you aren't roaming the streets and getting into trouble. Plus, I see here that you have been named valedictorian of your junior high school class. Your probation counselor also informed me of your family situation."

The judge had given Reggie a stern look as he scratched his chin. He paused before continuing. "I'm going to dismiss the charges." He hesitated. "Provided you get your butt back in school, graduate junior high, and attend high school." He paused again. "But not the high school in your neighborhood. There's another school that I have in mind. One with an aggressive and advanced curriculum that is geared toward challenging kids like you, keeping you in the books and not on the streets. I've signed off on the paperwork, so when you graduate from junior high—you will graduate, young man, am I right?"

Reggie had nodded.

"Good, then you will be automatically enrolled. If I ever see you in my courtroom again, son, I'm sending you straight to reform school or prison. Do you understand me?"

Reggie was shaking but had managed to say, "Yes, sir."

The judged had slammed his gavel down and said, "Case dismissed."

That had been the day, even though he was only fourteen years old, that he had decided to take advantage of the opportunity given to him. The judge was right in that he was a smart kid. Even though he had to hang out with some of the "bad guys" whenever he came home, he had always loved to go to school every day. School was his sanctuary, the one place where he could relax, learn, and feel safe for a few hours of the day. He loved to read, and some days he would purposely stay late and go to the school library to read books and do his homework before going home. On the weekends, he more often than not would scrounge up enough money to take D.C transit down to the big public library. There he would spend almost an entire day browsing through all sorts of books, many of which he would check out with his library card.

He did graduate from junior high and went to the special high school where he managed to play baseball, which for the most part kept him out of trouble in the hood. He ultimately graduated with honors. He had planned to attend college on a baseball scholarship, but his mother had been laid off from her job cleaning offices at night. His father, who was in and out of the family's life, had had a heart attack and couldn't get a job. Money became tighter, and his mother had to request additional assistance from welfare.

After graduation, because he was the oldest, he had had to put college on hold to help out the family. He tried his hand at construction, hauling plaster, cement, and bricks. It was backbreaking work, but when there was work, it brought in extra money, always cash because he was just a teenager. Times had been tough then and it was difficult for a teenager to find steady, good-paying work. He had found himself with no real sense of direction and slowly sliding back down that path of illegal activity.

It was all around him: numbers, gambling, drugs, and prostitution. He had even once considered being a pimp. Then the Vietnam War had started. The draft and maybe the war were the best things that could have happened to him at the time, getting him off the streets. He sighed and halted his reverie. *And here I am,* he thought.

He looked at his watch again and decided he'd pack it in. He picked up his briefcase and thought about

Friday night in D.C. and his pending trip back to the hood where he would have to stay for more than fifteen minutes. He cursed himself for feeling that way because his family loved him, and they were still there. But deep down that burning desire and promise to himself that he would never go back still haunted him.

CHAPTER 35

The old neighborhood looked the same. The years that had passed hadn't changed it much. He had been back a few times since he got his new job with the corporation, but he only stayed to see his mother and siblings for fifteen- to twenty-minute stretches at a time. Even when he had to use his sister, Autumn, to ride with him to repossess cars, he would call her in advance and swing through to pick her up as fast as he could. He would just honk, and Autumn would come running out. He did notice that there seemed to be more cars than usual parked in front of the red-brick duplex apartments. He guessed that the residents had gotten tired of riding D.C. transit and found a way to buy cars. Probably a few had hit the numbers and splurged with their winnings.

He pulled his 'Vette in front of his mother's duplex. Two of his younger sisters who were sitting on the front steps waved at him and rushed toward his car. Of course, they had seen it before, but he knew why they were excited. He had promised them that he would take them for a ride. But with five sisters and one at a time, it would be a long process. Especially since he didn't come around to visit very often. His younger brother, Jermaine, came out of the house, shook his hand, and slapped him on the back.

"Hey, big brother, everyone is out back waiting for you."

Reggie grabbed the two cases of beer on his front seat. His brother picked up the three bottles of Old Crow and a couple of bottles of wine.

As they walked through the small living area and kitchen of the house, he could see several people out the backdoor. He spotted his mother near the barbeque grill. When she realized that he had arrived, she turned and embraced him with a kiss.

"I made you your favorite potato salad and baked beans, and I'm about to start up the ribs and chicken."

Reggie shook his head and said, "Ma, you can't afford this."

His mother just waved her hand and smiled. "This is for my oldest child, and I'm so proud of you, Reggie."

He decided not to argue and just enjoy the moment with his mother and family. He also knew that he would do what he always did when he left. He would slip into her bedroom, go over to her dresser, find the drawer where she stashed her pocketbook, and put in two or three twenties with a note saying, "I love you."

CHAPTER 36

The party was uneventful from Reggie's perspective. However, lots of neighbors, friends, and relatives had stopped by to wish him well and talk to his mother, brother, and sisters. A couple of the neighborhood women flirted with him. He made a point to be polite but not take the bait. At around midnight, the party started to wind down. He checked his watch and went back inside the house to peek out the front window. It was an old habit. His 'Vette was still there. He was pretty sure that everyone in the neighborhood knew his car, but he didn't want to become too relaxed. His four little sisters had done a good job of watching it for him. He smiled when he thought about the fact that it was going to cost him five dollars each for their services.

He was getting a little tired as he looked at his watch again while thinking about how he was going to tell his mother that he was ready to leave. He didn't notice that Autumn had come up behind him. She poked him in the back.

"Hey, big brother. It looks like you are winding down and looking for a way to get out of here. I haven't had a chance to talk to you all evening."

Reggie turned around. "Yeah, it's been a long day. I've been meaning to come by the house one evening after work, but—"

She cut him off. "Yeah, yeah. Promises, promises. Hey, but I understand. You are Mr. Big Shot now and very busy."

Reggie knew she was playing him. "Hey, sis, you know that I miss you guys and . . . "

"Hey, no need to apologize, big bro. We are all very proud of you. You are still the motivation that we all can get out of here." She pointed around. "One day."

Reggie didn't respond. They looked at each other for a moment. Autumn broke the silence.

"So how's your love life these days?"

Reggie shrugged. "You know nothing special. Just doing my thing."

Autumn nodded. "Just thought I'd ask. I couldn't help but notice Denise and Carla were all over you tonight."

"Yeah, I know, but you know I'm not going back down those roads."

Autumn laughed. "Yeah, I don't blame you." She looked at him sheepishly.

He noticed and asked, "What?"

"Oh, nothing."

"Hey, don't give me that 'oh, nothing.' What?"

She hesitated before responding. "Well, I wanted to ask: had you talked to Tracey lately?"

Reggie stepped back a little and said, "Whoa . . . Whoa, little sister. Where did that come from?"

Autumn hunched her shoulders. "Hey, I just asked."

"You know that's over, right?" he continued with the slight admonishment. "Yeah, the last thing I heard was that she married her boyfriend from college. He's some kind of an attorney or something. So I'm not going there."

Autumn smiled and stepped closer to him. "So you see that's why I'm your favorite oldest little sister." She added, "But let's keep it simple, I look out for my big brother."

"And what is that supposed to mean?"

"Since you have been living 'across the river' and not stopping by lately, you've missed out on all the juicy gossip."

"Like what?"

"Like Ms. Tracey is no longer married."

He looked at her but said nothing.

"She's divorced, and she's living with her mother right now. She's transferred schools, but she's still teaching."

Although he was trying hard not to show any visual signs of emotion, Autumn knew her brother well enough to know she had gotten his attention.

"As a matter of fact, she's teaching at Eisenhower Elementary School. You know, over on 5th Street."

Autumn said no more. She knew it was time to wait for him. She held her breath and asked herself, *Would he explode and really go off or what?*

Reggie had taken Autumn's comments regarding Tracey in with great trepidation. He wanted to say, "Serves her right." But another part of him was saying, *Man, now's your chance to get her back.*

Autumn couldn't quite tell which way her brother was going to sway. She thought about changing the subject, stepping away, and leaving him be. But she had one more piece of information to tell him, and then it would be out of her hands and up to him.

"Well, I guess you are wondering how I came across this bit of information?"

He just looked at her and said nothing.

She pursed her lips, cocked her head to one side, and put her hands on her hips. "Well, I was at the beauty shop a few days ago and lo and behold, Ms. Tracey walked in, and of course after the small talk, she asked about you and how you were doing."

Reggie stepped away and took a few paces across the room. He didn't know why, but his legs were weakening. He turned and came back toward his little sister and managed to say, "So?"

"So, I told her all about my big brother and his big-time job."

A couple of neighbors entered the room and said hello. Reggie politely acknowledged them as he gently grabbed Autumn's arm and pulled her off to the side whispering, "So is that it?"

"Gee, Reggie, give me a break. I didn't have to tell you anything, you know."

He caught himself and let her arm go. "I'm sorry."

Autumn rubbed her arm and looked him squarely in the eyes before saying, "Okay I accept your apology. Now may I continue?" Reggie nodded.

"Anyway, she gave me her phone number and asked that I give it to you." She shyly added, "Perhaps you might wish to call her when you find the time from your important job."

She smirked, and Reggie gritted his teeth.

"Oh, so I'm supposed to call her, huh? Why didn't you just give her my phone number and tell her to call me?"

"Hey, big brother, don't kill the messenger."

He stared at her and realized that he shouldn't direct his anger toward her. He took a moment to control his rapid breathing. Autumn looked at him.

"So do you want her phone number or what?"

He had to smile at her. He knew she had him right where she wanted. That was the special bond that they had. She could read him like a book. He also had to admit that the possibility of talking to Tracey again was intriguing. But he knew he could not admit to anyone, not even to Autumn, that he had lain awake countless nights, wondering what went wrong between him and Tracey. He extended his hand. "Alright, give me the number."

She smiled and slapped a piece of paper in his hand and headed back to the kitchen. She turned as she was leaving the room, watching Reggie stare at the piece of paper. She flippantly said, "Good luck, big brother. Oh, and by the way, she looked good. I mean really good."

CHAPTER 37

Reggie paced the living room area of his apartment. He checked his watch for the one-thousandth time. He still had over an hour to go. He went back into his hallway and looked in the full-length mirror on the wall. He stepped back and turned around to make sure his pants were pressed right. The crease was crisp. He tucked his shirt in and was satisfied with the way he looked. In an hour he had to look his best, he thought.

The restaurant was only twenty minutes away in downtown D.C., and at this time of day, traffic would not present a problem, except maybe for trying to find a parking space. He thought about the parking and decided he had better leave early and allow the extra time. He'd rather be there early because he wasn't one of those fashionably late folks. He checked his watch again, went back into his living room, picked up his suit jacket, and left his apartment. He smiled as he approached his sharp-looking 'Vette parked out front. He had gotten up early in the morning and pulled it into the alley behind his apartment and washed and waxed it. As he got in behind the wheel, he thought about what he would say. Things had happened so fast. He wasn't sure how he had gotten to this point. All he knew was that the little voice in his head kept telling him that he had to do it. He had to make the call.

It had been a couple of days since he had gotten the courage to call her, but he had managed to pick up the phone and dialed her number. He was lucky because Tracey, not her mother, picked up on the third ring. He remembered there was a moment of hesitation when he heard her voice. He almost hung the phone up because his heart began to thump in his chest. She had to say hello several times before he spoke. Then there was silence on her end before she spoke.

She had begun the conversation by telling him that she thought he would never call. That sort of broke the ice, and he had been able to keep the conversation going. However, he remembered it had been very brief. And now, he was pulling away from his apartment and heading downtown to meet Tracey for lunch still thinking to himself, *What will I say?*

As he had anticipated, the drive to the restaurant was short. He had no problem getting there, and he was pleased that he was early. He had forgotten that the restaurant had valet parking, and this pleased him even more. For the most part, he wouldn't have to worry about someone dinging his car. He gave the valet parker five dollars to ensure he would take extra care of his 'Vette.

He walked into the busy restaurant, smiling momentarily as he passed several attractive ladies standing in the lobby. He knew that they had seen him roll up in the 'Vette, and the nod of the head and smile was just him completing his grand entrance. For some reason, he felt he still had to play the part. He said hello and flashed his million-dollar smile as he passed them and headed to the bar. He needed a beer to calm down and collect himself.

Even with the beer, it was still tough to stop his hands from trembling and his heart from racing. His mind was a total blank as he was going over and over what he would say. He had never had this confusing feeling before. His thoughts were interrupted as he spotted Tracey entering the restaurant and being directed to the bar. As she entered the bar area, their eyes met, his heart pounded and he felt like he was looking at a supermodel. She was wearing a very short black cocktail dress and hoop earrings, and her hair was pressed straight and hung down to her shoulders. She looked absolutely stunning. Several men at the bar stopped their conversation to look at her. He had to keep his cool. He quickly jumped up from the bar stool and stood to greet her.

"Hello, Tracey. You look great."

"Hello, Reggie. So do you."

"Can I get you a drink?"

"Okay, I'll have a Vodka Collins."

Reggie turned, "Mr. Bartender."

CHAPTER 38

They were about halfway through their drinks when the maître d' came into the bar to escort them to their table. He was somewhat relieved to take a break from the conversation, which so far had been very vanilla, just the usual chitchat. They both were keeping the conversation light and very general.

Every now and then, he would catch himself staring at her and telling himself how good she really looked.

He could hear her talking, but his mind was in another world. He would nod his head but have no idea what she had just said. He could only hope that he was nodding at the right thing.

As they were waiting for their lunch, he ordered two more drinks to hopefully loosen things up. When the drinks arrived, he clinked their glasses and said, "Cheers."

After seeing the smile on her face, he added, "So why did you want to see me?"

Tracey put down her drink and replied, "What do you mean, see you? Why did you want to see me?"

Reggie could feel the electricity and sensed the direction of the conversation. He sat back in his chair and put down his drink. "Okay, so why did you give Autumn your phone number to give to me?"

Tracey squirmed a little, sensing negativity, but said, "Because Autumn said you wanted my number."

Reggie rolled his eyes and thought to himself, *I'm going to kill her; I'm going to kill my little sister.*

"Okay, Tracey. Let's just for a moment forget the whys. Let's look at the fact that we are here and there must be a reason. I'm here because . . . " He shook his head. "I don't know. All I know is that I wanted to be here to see you." He shook his head again. "I don't know."

Tracey looked at him but said nothing. She too was going through a lot seeing him for the first time since that dreadful day at college. Up until this point, she had managed to keep her anxiety level low, but she knew she was losing it now. Ever since he had called her, she had wondered what she would say to him.

To say she was sorry just didn't seem like much of an apology. Several times she had told herself just to leave it be. *Don't bring it up. It's too late. What's done is done. Get on with your life. He's gone forever.* She thought about all the men she had met since her divorce. They were all of little interest to her.

Nowadays, the only satisfaction she got was raising her daughter. She reflected on how narrow her life had gotten with no real direction. She had to face the reality that she was not happy with the single life, but somehow she had managed to survive. It wasn't just a coincidence that she walked into the beauty shop that day. She had known Autumn would be there getting her hair done. She broke off her thoughts because their lunch had arrived.

So they did the natural thing and began to eat. Reggie was still confused, not knowing where he was emotionally. He felt angry enough to think that he could just forget her and walk away, but he also knew deep down that there was still something there. While eating, he thought, *She still hasn't said anything. It's like she's hasn't heard a word I've said.*

The food and extra drinks had not done the trick. Tracey still wasn't feeling very comfortable. Deep down, she had wanted this opportunity to happen. She knew she needed to finally get *it* out there. She just couldn't figure out how or when. Not until the dessert had been ordered and the waitress was leaving their table did she convince herself that it was now or never.

"Reggie, look, I have something to say. Something to just get out there. I've been harboring this for a long time now, and the only way I can say it is to just say I'm sorry."

He knew what she meant, but he wanted to hear more. "Sorry about what?"

"Okay, okay, you aren't going to make this easy, are you?"

He just stared at her.

"Alright then. I'm sorry for ending our relationship when I was in college. I know now that it was a mistake and that I probably hurt you. You probably won't believe this, but I didn't find out until after I was married that you actually did write to me when you were in Vietnam."

Reggie was utterly amazed by her statement. "Wait a minute. Why after you were married? You didn't believe me when I pleaded that I had—"

She held up her hand to cut him off.

"It's a long story, Reggie, but I guess there's no better time than now to tell you. It was my mother and—"

Reggie cut her off. "Yeah, right."

"No, I'm telling you the truth. Just hear me out. My parents, I'm sure you remember, never really liked you and what neighborhood you were from. They were not happy when they learned that I was seeing you. So when I went off to college and you to Vietnam, well, they felt the distance and me being away from you would take its toll and end the relationship."

Reggie stirred a little in his chair.

Tracey continued, "So when your letters started to come to our house, my father told my mother not to forward them to me at school. He actually told her to just burn them. While my mother didn't really care that much about you, she did somehow realize how I felt about you and for some reason never burned your letters. She just kept them."

Reggie sarcastically said, "Yeah, but she never forwarded them either."

Tracey shook her head but did not respond. She continued, "Anyway, as you may have heard, my father passed away last year. One day over lunch, I was talking with my mom about my failed marriage, my dad, etc. Out of the blue, she goes out to her car in the parking lot and comes back with this shoebox with all the letters you sent me. I read them all, Reggie, and what else can I say? I'm sorry I didn't believe you at the time. I'm—"

Reggie had heard enough and put up his hands. "Oh, come on, Tracey. You expect me to believe that cock-and-bull story. You are blaming this all on your parents?" His voice became a little higher as he shook his head. "Even if they did do that—and that's still a big if in my book--didn't you even just once think about our relationship before you went off to college? Didn't you remember how in love we were? At least that's what I thought. How could you think I would just go off to Vietnam and not ever try to contact you? Why didn't you stop by mother's house to get my mailing address or talk to my brother or Autumn to contact me?"

He was riled up now. "Come on, Tracey, let's call it like it is. You saw the opportunity to dump me and run off to college with your parent's approved highfalutin' friends." He threw his napkin on the table. "Just admit it."

Tracey was in tears and got up from the table. The waitress had returned with their desserts. She turned to the waitress and said, "I won't be having dessert."

She looked at Reggie. "And as for you, Reginald Saunders, I tried to be honest with you, and I apologized. Everything that I have said was the truth. But I see now that you still haven't grown up. Maybe you are right in your cavalier assessment of me. Yeah, maybe we can't go back there. Have a good life in Detroit, Mr. Saunders."

She left the table. Reggie had already cursed himself for his outburst and tried to halt her, but she was gone before he could get up. The puzzled waitress was still standing there with their dessert orders.

He sat back and said, "I'll take the check." He handed one of the desserts back to the waitress. "And I guess dessert is on me."

CHAPTER 39

DETROIT, MICHIGAN
THE PHOENIX PROGRAM

The conference room looked bare. At least that's what Reggie thought as he surveyed it. He was seated at a large table centered in the room. There were exactly ten chairs arranged around the table. Although he was on the twenty-first floor of Nation's Automotive Financial Corporation Headquarters, he had noticed that this room had no windows, just the four walls around him and the door that he had entered through earlier. *Rather nondescript,* he thought as he looked down at the pad of lined paper in front of him and the pen with the company's logo on it. There was a slight stir in the room as he broke his train of thought and looked around at the other nine individuals seated at the table. He smiled again at the person seated next to him on his right. He had said good morning earlier and asked his name. *Hector, Hector Perez,* he thought. He had also said good morning to a Jason Montgomery and Sam Woo. Everyone seemed nice enough as they introduced themselves and asked each other where they were from, how long they had been with the corporation, exactly why they were there, and so on. The odd thing that struck Reggie was that no one seemed to know why exactly they were there. The only other thing that stood out to him within the group was that there was not a white person in the room—ten people of color or some non-white ethnic background. *Interesting*, he thought, but he didn't make any more of it.

The general chatter among the group was interrupted when the door of the room swung open and two well-dressed men entered followed by a woman carrying several folders. The woman immediately went around the table, placing the folders in front of each individual. The taller of the two men approached the head of the table and said, "Thank you, Cathy. That will be all for now."

He faced the group and introduced himself.

"Good morning, gentlemen. My name is Chris Roden. I am the director of Human Resources. I'm in charge and have the overall responsibility for what we are calling the Phoenix Program." He pointed to the other man. "This is my assistant, Greg Morton. He will be your supervisor and the person to whom you will be directly reporting during your stay here at headquarters. Now, if you would turn your attention to the folder in front of you."

Roden waited until the stir of the folders being picked up quieted down and then he continued. "You have been selected to participate in this innovative program because your employment histories, coupled with strong individual performance evaluations by your respective field office managers, suggest that you have great future potential. The Phoenix Program has been designed to provide you with the necessary skills and expertise to take on senior management responsibilities. I'm sure you are aware that Nation's Automotive Financial Corporation is a multi-national conglomerate. In this program, you will be exposed to other areas and business opportunities of the corporation that you may not be aware of…things such as international subsidiaries, manufacturing, accounting, personnel, loans, and banking, just to name a few. In other words, in two years, all of you, if you successfully complete the program, will become senior managers at one of over 400 corporate field locations. You will be managing over 200 employees per location. Each of you came from one of those field locations. You will become the man in that corner office. You will have a salary commensurate with your individual field office size. The larger the field office, the more you will make. In addition, you will become what we call 'Bonus Eligible.' This means you will be eligible to share in the success of the corporation. If the corporation is profitable and exceeds its financial goals, then you will receive an annual cash sum over and above your base salary. You will also receive a company car, and if you are married, your wife will receive a company car. Sorry, gentlemen, if you are unmarried, your girlfriend will not receive a company car."

There was a little laughter from the group. Roden paused for another moment. There was an obvious stir as everyone looked at each other. Reggie was beside himself. He couldn't believe what he was hearing. *This is crazy*, he thought.

When the room quieted down again, Roden added, "There is another thing that we have incorporated into the program. If you turn to page twelve of your folder, it will explain an integral part of the program. It's what we call the Oversee Board. This will be a monthly evaluation of your retention and comprehension through a series of questions and real-life scenarios. There's a lot of training, information, and material that you will be exposed to during your two years here. Gentlemen, make no mistake about it. It's going to be hard and fast and perhaps overwhelming at times. The Oversee Board component of the program will allow us, the evaluators, to determine whether or not you move on to the next phase of the program. The Oversee Board will be comprised of senior department heads from various areas of headquarters. You might also anticipate a vice president to be a panel member and sit in on one of your Oversee Board assignments. He might ask you questions and weigh in on your evaluation."

Roden paused and looked around the table. "And gentlemen, I will be blunt here. Yes, you have been selected for this program, but this is not an automatic or free pass. If you do not pass these Oversee Boards, you will be dismissed from the program and be reassigned back to the field."

The room was quieter than quiet. Reggie's excitement went down several notches, as he thought about the possibility of being sent back to a Field Office. He definitely did not want that to happen.

Roden still had everyone's attention and added, "There is one more thing that I will briefly mention, and it is not in your folder. We have another group of individuals here at headquarters that you will be working and interfacing with. These individuals as of yet have none of the field experience all of you have. We have recruited them directly from some of the most elite universities in the country, universities such as Harvard, Yale, Princeton, Wharton, and Stanford. They all have their undergraduate degrees and have or are working on their MBAs. If they are successful in headquarters, they are projected to be our future leaders."

Roden stared at the group before summarizing. "Finally, all that I will add is, gentlemen, this is your opportunity of a lifetime. Take advantage of it. Now, before I turn you over to Greg, any questions?"

Everyone in the group looked around at each other. Reggie had a question but wasn't sure he should ask it.

Then he just said to himself, *What the hell!*

He was always taught that he didn't know unless he asked. He raised his hand and Roden acknowledged him.

"Uh, sir. You mentioned this other group from the, uh, elite universities that we will be working with on certain assignments."

"Yes."

"Will they be subject to these Oversee Boards?"

Roden looked at the group and then glanced at Morton. "No."

Reggie looked over at Hector Perez, who stared straight ahead. Reggie felt like he was on an island when it was apparent that Roden was not going to elaborate, but he managed to say, "Uh, thank you, sir."

Greg Morton immediately jumped in and said, "Thanks for your time, Mr. Roden."

"Okay, gentlemen, we have a lot to cover, so let's get started. Turn back to page two in your folders."

CHAPTER 40

"**G**ood morning, gentlemen. I hope you looked over your folders last night and then got a good night's sleep." Greg Morton looked around the room at the ten individuals. "Today is day two of possibly the rest of your career with the corporation."

Everyone was sitting in the same chairs as they had the day before. Reggie glanced over at Hector Perez, who this time glanced back and smiled.

Morton continued. "Today, you will be receiving your individual assignments, but before I hand them out to you, I wanted to give you what I deem to be pertinent information on how to get your minds set to navigate this program."

"First of all, as you have been informed, this is a two-year training program. However, you should consider it a two-year job, because you will be receiving your regular salaries every two weeks. So that means from headquarters' perspective, it's like any other job. You will report to work each morning, work your butts off, and then go home in the evenings and are free to do whatever you want. However, I would strongly recommend that you use the time wisely. Studying should be at the top of your to-do lists." Morton paused before continuing, "Secondly, I'm the facilitator of the program. I will steer you through your assignments, set them up, etc. If you have any problems or questions, you will clear them through me. In essence, I will be responsible for you throughout the two years, hopefully, that you are here. Now some helpful hints to get you acclimated."

He spread his arms. "This is corporate headquarters. It is indeed flashy, and some might say glamorous compared to the field where you all came from. But you gentlemen will not be participating in that part. You will basically be in the dungeon of this building and only surfacing when called upon. So don't get caught up in the 'ooh and ahh.' My best advice would be to stay focused, humble, and unseen."

Morton walked around the table, eyeing everyone as he continued, "Now I did mention dungeon, but that might be a little exaggerated. I just wanted to get your attention. Your new home, where you will be reporting to each morning, is affectionately called 'the Corral.' It's where your day will begin and end. Actually, it's really not in the basement. It's on the second floor of the building. They put it there just in case anyone decided to jump. They figured you wouldn't get hurt too badly."

Everyone laughed.

"Actually, the Corral is right down the hall from the vice presidents' suites and offices, which means you will be in the company of approximately twenty vice presidents each and every day while you are in the building."

There was a noticeable murmur around the table.

"You each will be assigned one vice president and will report directly to him each morning. The purpose of this one-on-one, as Mr. Roden elaborated, is for you to learn from the people who are the movers and shakers and who make the decisions within the corporation."

Morton walked around the table, passing out the assignments while still speaking. "Gentlemen, you will learn from these men and what they do. You will do whatever they ask. If they say 'Jump,' you had better say, 'How high?'"

The group laughed again. Reggie immediately thought of boot camp.

"And gentlemen, if you haven't guessed by now, make no mistake about it. This is a competition. Each of you will be evaluated and judged individually. The powers that be want to see who rises to the top, plain and simple. As I said, I will be available whenever you need me and will guide you as best as I can. But at this point, it's really up to you. Any questions?"

No one raised their hand.

Morton looked around, then picked up his things. "Okay then— follow me. We are headed to your new home in the building, the Corral."

CHAPTER 41

Ten pairs of eyes stared into the large, windowless room. There were two rows of long tables in the middle. Each table had small partitions evenly spaced to separate what appeared to be individual workstations. Between each partition were a chair, computer, and phone. Reggie did the math: five workstations on each of the two tables for a total of ten workstations. Additionally, he and his fellow trainees observed ten other cubicles lined around the walls of the room. Each cubicle was partitioned and in each sat an individual. Reggie and the others in his group looked in puzzlement at the ten men who had not turned around when they entered the room. The men all seemed preoccupied with whatever they were doing. Reggie shrugged his shoulders and walked into the room with the rest of his group. He was anticipating some sort of introduction to the other ten men, but as he and his group dispersed to their assigned workstations, Morton said nothing. Two of the nameless men briefly turned around, rolled their eyes, and resumed their prior positions, backs toward Reggie's group. After his group found their respective stations, Morton informed them that they had about an hour to get set up and operational. Reggie got seated and looked around the room again, thinking to himself that maybe the "Dungeon" was a better name for his so-called new home.

After an hour or so and by working together, Reggie's group had managed to get all their computers up and running. However, everyone couldn't help but notice that the other ten men seated at their workstations had not offered to help or introduce themselves. Reggie wondered why. He decided that maybe he would take the first step and initiate the introductions.

He walked over to one of the men who had briefly turned around earlier, tapped him on the shoulder, and said, "Hi, my name is Reggie Saunders, and we—"

Before he could finish his introduction, the man turned around as well as the other nine men in unison.

"Yeah, we know who you are."

Reggie was taken aback by his hostile tone but said, "Okay then. Who are you?" And as he asked the question, he looked briefly at the other nine men.

The guy that Reggie was addressing said, "I'm Roger Hempfell, and we—"

Before he could continue, Reggie interrupted and said, "Yeah, we know who you are. You are the new hires to corporate headquarters."

Hempfell nodded and grinned as he said, "Yeah, I guess we are going to be seeing a lot of each other." Then he turned around as did the other nine men.

Reggie took the hint and walked back over to Hector Perez, Sam Woo, Jason Montgomery, and the rest of the group who were standing by their workstations. He smiled, held his hands up, and said, "Gentle-men, let the games begin."

CHAPTER 42

THE PHOENIX PROGRAM

"**S**aunders, this is crap."

Jack Kramer threw the two sheets of paper across his desk to Reggie who was standing in front of him.

"I need this to be concise and to the point. You are rambling here. I have made the corrections. So take it and get it cleaned up."

Reggie, mumbling to himself, exited Kramer's office. He had spent all night and the wee hours of the prior morning drafting what he thought was the perfect memo and Jack—Jack Kramer, the vice president of everything (in his own eyes)—had just torn it to shreds in less than one minute. Of course, he should not have been surprised as he walked back to the Corral. Working for Kramer had been hell thus far. It was just his luck to be assigned to someone named Jack. Not short for Jackson or another name for John, just Jack. Who would name their kid just Jack? Anyway, Jack Kramer was a hard-driving egomaniac in Reggie's opinion. The guy just couldn't be pleased or satisfied with anything he presented to him. But Reggie had made up his mind a few months into his ordeal. He wasn't going to let Jack bring him down. He had decided to do whatever it took to hang in there and somehow get this dude off his back.

He had already adjusted his arrival time to get to work. Kramer came to the office around seven-thirty each morning. Reggie made it a point to be there by six-thirty. Plus, he made sure he bought Kramer a cup of coffee (with money from his own pocket) and placed it on a table outside his office each morning just before he arrived. He learned that tip from Kramer's secretary, Melissa, whom he had befriended and spoke to from time to time. She seemed friendly enough, but she probably just felt sorry for him. This coffee thing, black coffee only, was an expected ritual. Some sort of "rite of passage" that Kramer demanded. And so it went for what seemed an eternity. Reggie did everything he could to learn and anticipate whatever Kramer wanted him to do and do it right the first time.

Although Kramer had not verbally eased up, Reggie felt that he was slowly making progress. The memos being returned from him had fewer red markings, strikeouts, and comments. He finally began to feel that waking up at five each morning to be able to make it to work by six-thirty, including the commute, was paying off, even if only from the standpoint that he was always there when Kramer arrived each morning. He also made it a point, no matter how late, that he was always there when Kramer walked out at night. He learned that Kramer, not surprisingly, had been married three times and was currently divorced. The evenings that he was at the office late was just a ruse. He most often would be up on the forty-fifth floor in the executives' lounge having drinks or dinner before leaving work. Then he would come back down to his office between six and six-thirty and pick up his briefcase before leaving the building. He would pass by the Corral door, briefly glance in and see Reggie at his workstation, but he would never say a word. This routine wreaked havoc with Reggie's sleep and his now non-existent social life, but it was a small victory. He knew he needed to remain focused and committed. He forced himself to look at the long term and hang in there for a shot at the big prize.

He was able to get some relief on the weekends because for whatever reason, working on the weekends or holidays was a rarity in corporate headquarters. He took advantage of that and was able to find a small, furnished apartment in a suburb just north of the city. It just had the basics: a bedroom, television, small kitchenette, and a living room with a small sofa, a chair, and a bathroom. The rent was reasonable, and it fit his needs, especially when he considered the fact that during the week, he just slept there. He was putting in ten to twelve hours a day at headquarters. The location of the apartment was great because there were plenty of nearby stores and restaurants. On the weekends when he wasn't too tired, he would occasionally catch up with Hector, Sam, and Jason at a bar or restaurant, down a few beers, and compare notes on the vice presidents and the program. It seemed like everyone else had normal vice presidents. They all jokingly agreed that Reggie must have pissed someone off to get Jack Kramer.

CHAPTER 43

Reggie felt that things couldn't get any worse, except there was the politics of the Corral. It was very obvious to him that there was a double standard taking shape. Roger Hempfell and his fellow MBAs were the chosen ones from elite universities. Reggie's group was relegated to the bottom of the corporate ladder: the trainees. During the months that followed, it was evident that Hempfell was the leader of the "Boys" or "Cronies," as Reggie called them, and that Reggie had taken up the gauntlet for his group.

Hempfell or one of his boys never wasted a moment in reminding him, Hector, Sam, or Jason that they didn't have college degrees. So how were they ever going to manage a field office with several hundred employees or become vice presidents? This angered him to no end because he knew they were partially correct in that no one in corporate headquarters or a field office would ever take him seriously unless he had a degree, a four-year degree. Even with a four-year degree, he still had to face the reality that he and the rest of his group had been selected due to some Affirmative Action initiative. He had read in one of his business books back in community college that some of the major companies were moving in the direction of diversity in their workforces. Deep down, he felt privileged that he could take advantage of what the Phoenix Program obviously represented. Greg Morton had explained to him on several occasions that the program was designed to give him and the others a "jump start" in management. While Reggie sincerely appreciated the objective behind the program, he would counter to Greg that he and the rest of the group could still be productive and could be managers without the "jump start" if only they didn't face so many roadblocks and subtle discriminations. Speaking of his own plight, yes, had he had a better childhood and upbringing and if a war had not broken out and had he gone on to college, maybe he and Greg wouldn't be having this discussion. He would also add that if the playing field were level, he could succeed and become whatever he wanted to be, even within Nation's Automotive Financial Corporation.

Greg would ultimately end the discussion by patting Reggie on the shoulder and saying something like, "Yes, Reggie, in a perfect world, there would not be a need for the Phoenix Program, but unfortunately, the reality is that there is a glass ceiling that precludes minorities from breaking through. That's the real corporate world. However, I can assure you that the men behind the Phoenix Program firmly believe in trying to 'right' the obvious 'wrong.' It's not going to happen overnight, but you and the rest of the group are a start."

Greg would smile and then add, "So hang in there and don't make us regret our decision."

Even with all the negatives, Reggie still felt that the men who went through the Phoenix Program would dispel some of that corporate bias and make a difference.

Meanwhile, Hempfell and his boys were relentless in sticking it in Reggie and the others' faces. When the vice presidents weren't looking or listening, Hempfell and his group were always using Affirmative Action in some of their verbal sparring to suggest they were not truly deserving. Reggie would counter by asking Hempfell or any of his boys had they ever collected a delinquent account in person or repossessed a car. That usually shut them down for a minute or two. However, Hempfell would always fall back on taunting that they would be vice presidents someday and would just instruct the staff—the Reggies, Sams, Hectors, and Jasons who worked for them—to get the job done. In other words, they could learn the job from the top down.

Reggie would just shake his head and say to himself, *Sure, you can.*

But still it bothered him that he didn't have a four-year college degree. It was insane to think he could find the time, but he thought about it hard and long, and he decided he had to make the sacrifice. In his mind, it was the only way to stop the constant barrage from Hempfell and people like him, like that prick Lattimore. So he enrolled in night classes. He did the math and determined that with his associates degree, he had two years already toward the four years that he needed. He realized that it would be tough taking business school night classes with all the required reading of books, books, and more books, but he felt fortunate in that he always loved books and reading, so he could make it work.

The inner feuds in the Corral between the two groups continued throughout the first year with no sign of letting up. It was difficult avoiding outright confrontation, but Reggie persuaded all his guys to just keep their cool and find a way to get through the program. He coached them to complete the program and then go out to the field and make a difference. Prove them wrong.

Meanwhile, he still had to deal with Jack Kramer's every whim. He had managed to keep ahead of him, and everything thus far had gone as planned from his perspective. He even had aced all the Oversee Boards that they had put him through. Sometimes he would stay up all night and into the wee hours of the morning studying and preparing for the onslaught of questions and scenarios. It was always a great feeling to get his report from Greg Morton that he had passed and would be going on to the next phase of the program. It was also a disappointing thought that he, Hector, Sam, Jason, and the rest of the group had to go through what amounted to pure hell while Roger Hempfell and his group just skated along with no pressure whatsoever. It was a bitter pill to swallow, but he realized that this whole corporate politics stuff, in the end, was much bigger than him. He just had to keep plowing through all the obstacles and roadblocks to get to the end of the race.

CHAPTER 44

DETROIT CORPORATE HEADQUARTERS

Chris Roden eased back into his chair, took off his glasses, and placed them on his desk. He wiped his forehead with his handkerchief. Earlier, he had summoned Greg Morton to meet with him for a brief update on the program. It had been over a year, and from his perspective, everything regarding the Phoenix Program had gone relatively well. He had reported several times to his boss, Daniel Hartsdale, who had kept Curtis Livingston, the chairman and president of the board, happy with the success of the program.

Greg Morton quietly gave a tap on Roden's door and entered his office.

"Morning, Chris."

"Good morning, Greg. Anything new?"

Morton smiled and said, "No, not really. Nothing that we haven't anticipated. Our boys still haven't killed each other yet. As you know, it took a while for everyone to settle in and figure out who's who, but things are moving along. You can feel the underlying tension, but I must admit the field guys are holding their own with our college recruits. There's definitely an air of competitiveness between the two groups, and I guess that's a good thing. Lately, I've just been trying to keep the general peace and keep the interactions between them in-house and between you and me. No sense in getting Mr. Hartsdale involved."

Roden interjected, "Yeah, he's got enough on his plate dealing with running the operations side of a corporation and keeping the chairman and board at bay. Not to mention watching his back with Matthew Brenner and his cohorts."

The mention of Brenner reminded Morton that he wanted to update Roden on one more thing. "Uh, Chris, one more thing that I should mention."

Roden gave him a nod to continue.

"Brenner and one of his staff, John Parker, popped in unannounced at one of the Oversee Boards reviews and deliberately tried to trip up one of our trainees on a couple of questions."

This bit of news piqued Roden's attention, and he sat straight up in his chair, shook his head, and said, "Son of a . . . Who was the trainee?"

"It was Reginald Saunders, but don't worry. Saunders stumbled at first but managed to get back on track when he recounted a real-life field experience involving personally repossessing a car from a drug dealer. Brenner just huffed and walked out of the room."

Roden slid back in his chair and breathed a sigh of relief. "You serious?"

Morton smiled, nodded, and replied, "Yep, definitely went down like that." He added, "Don't worry, Chris. The Phoenix Program is a good program. It's been a long time coming and is way overdue. The men that we selected are going to make it through the program and go out and make a difference in the field. We both know Brenner, so we just have to stay out in front of him."

Roden relaxed and said, "Yeah, only a few more months to go before graduation. What a relief and accomplishment that will be."

Morton thought for a moment and then said, "I know the program will be over soon, and it's been a real grind, but I wish we could do a similar program up here in headquarters within some of the internal departments."

Roden nodded, but he added, "Yes, it would be nice and warranted, but like in the field, we don't have many minorities in headquarters. For instance, take our department, Human Resources. Who do we have? One or two personnel that may be promising?"

Morton nodded. "Well, we are getting a little better. We hired another promising young man a couple years ago who came up here to headquarters from the field. He's doing quite well."

Roden nodded again and asked, "What's his name?"

Morton responded, "Whitehead, Morris Whitehead."

Roden thought for a moment, but the name didn't ring a bell. He finally said, "Well, I guess that's a start."

CHAPTER 45

Morris Whitehead walked into his small cubicle and looked at personnel records on his desk. He had just gotten a cup of coffee from the break room and was starting another typical day at the office. Before sitting down to begin work, he stood a little longer and peered around the room at the 100 or so other employees. He smiled to himself and silently said, *I guess this is it. I've been here a couple years now. I'm comfortable. I know what I'm doing, and I like working here at Nation's Automotive Financial Corporation.* He realized now that it had been a good decision to accept a transfer and move to Detroit.

He sat down and thought about meeting his girlfriend, Sheila, for a happy hour drink and dinner later. He smiled again as he thought about the second big decision that he had made, which was to convince Sheila to come to Detroit and move in with him. It was difficult, and it all happened so fast, but in the end, she said yes. She had come, moved in, got a job, and so far everything was working out fine. However, before making the decision to ask her to come, he had had to make a few sacrifices. He threw away his little black book and put himself out of circulation. He had finally admitted to himself that Sheila was the one and only. He knew that it was only a matter of time before he would pop the question.

His thoughts were interrupted when a coworker passed by, patted him on the shoulder, and said, "Hey, Morris, don't forget we will be in the cafeteria for lunch today."

Morris turned around and said, "Yeah, no problem. I'll see you guys at noon."

CHAPTER 46

Reggie sat quietly by himself in the main cafeteria of corporate headquarters. Usually he ate lunch with Sam, Hector, Jason, and some others in a smaller lunchroom in the basement of the building. The smaller lunchroom was the group's chosen sanctuary to get away from the grinding day that they had to endure. However, the guys were out of the building on a training assignment, so he had decided rather than eat alone in the smaller cafeteria, he would venture up to the first floor main cafeteria. He figured that while he ate his lunch, he could watch all the frantic so-called movers and shakers bustle around and eat their lunches.

He had just sat down at a small table with his lunch when he heard a loud crashing sound. Someone had obviously dropped their lunch tray. He turned, as did several other employees, to see where the noise was coming from. Across the room, he observed a young man standing at a table looking totally embarrassed as his peers were laughing at what appeared to be a tray of food now on the floor. Reggie was somewhat amused as the young man was bending over to pick up his tray and said to himself, *Poor guy.* He watched a little longer and then hesitated. The young man looked familiar. He stared for a moment longer and then said to himself, *It can't be. No, it can't be.*

He gradually got out of his chair, walked over a little closer, and then said, "Morris?"

Morris Whitehead looked up at the man standing over him. He stopped what he was doing for a moment and stared at the man's face.

"Reggie?"

He immediately stood up and said, "I can't believe this. What are you doing here?"

Reggie quickly gave him a hug while saying, "Man, you are a sight for sore eyes. What are you doing here?"

Morris smiled and answered. "I work here."

Reggie replied, "No way. I work here, too."

Morris added, "Wow, I can't believe this. How long has it been?"

Reggie smiled and looked at him. "Too long, Morris, too long."

The other men at the table stirred a little, and Morris turned around and said, "Oh yeah, sorry. Let me introduce you to these guys who work with me."

After the quick introductions, Morris turned to Reggie and said, "Hey, look, man, we have so much to talk about and get caught up on . . . " As the other men were getting up from the table, Morris glanced at his watch and said, "But I have to get back to work."

He reached across the table, grabbed two napkins, pulled a pen from his pocket, and wrote his phone number and address down. He handed it to Reggie and asked him to write his phone number and address down on the other napkin. He said, "I'll give you a call later."

Reggie smiled as he watched Morris hurriedly leave the table to catch up with his coworkers. He shook his head in disbelief and thought, *Man, this is really unbelievable. Morris Whitehead and me working at the same company. Wow.*

CHAPTER 47

Sheila was sitting at dinner with Morris Whitehead. She couldn't help noticing that he was over-the-top excited ever since he picked her up from work. She couldn't get a word in edgewise while they drove to the restaurant. The entire conversation was about this Vietnam buddy he ran into at work. She briefly remembered that Morris had a photo of the two of them while they were in Vietnam, and she vaguely remembered the name Reggie, but that was about it. She hadn't seen Morris this excited since he asked her to move in with him.

They had just ordered when Morris said, "Oh, shoot. I forgot I was supposed to call him."

Sheila shook her head and said, "So?"

Morris smiled and said, "Hey, look, baby, I know this is all crazy, and I don't want to spoil dinner. So just let me step out for a minute, call him, and set something up for later." He winked. "Just so he knows I didn't forget him."

Sheila smiled at how wound up he was tonight.

Morris hurried to the vestibule area of the restaurant, found a phone, and dialed Reggie's phone number. Reggie answered on the first ring.

"Hey, Reggie. It's Morris. Look, I'm sorry, man, but I forgot that I had dinner set up with Sheila tonight and . . . "

Reggie interrupted, "Sheila?"

"Yeah, man, it's a long story. Anyway, I was planning on meeting up with you, but I'm going to have to give you a rain check, and I thought of something even better. What about dinner tomorrow night? Just you and me with no time restraints. We can really catch up on where the heck you've been. I know a fabulous restaurant. I can pick you up around six-thirty. How about it?"

Reggie was overwhelmed at the possibility of seeing Morris again and didn't hesitate to say, "Okay, man. You are on."

Morris replied, "Cool. I'll see you tomorrow night."

He hung up, sighed, and headed back to the table where he knew Sheila was going to ask him a thousand questions.

CHAPTER 48

Morris and Reggie arrived at a swanky restaurant called Fitzgerald's. They had been at the bar, frantically catching each other up on where they had been and how they got to Detroit. Neither could talk fast enough before the other would interrupt to ask questions. After their second drink at the bar, they headed for their table and sat down. The conversation shifted to the women now in their lives. Morris told Reggie all about Sheila. He recounted how he met her back home in Chicago and that they had both worked for Nation's Automotive Financial Corporation. They dated for a while, and then he got the transfer to Detroit. They had tried the long-distance romance thing, and it didn't work out. Since she couldn't get a transfer, he finally persuaded her to quit and move in with him. She eventually got another job in Detroit, and now they were happily living together. After another drink, he finally fessed up and admitted that she was the one. Reggie teased him a little because Morris had been the one who would never commit to a relationship and now here he was in love with only one woman. *Man*, he thought, *time and love can change a person.* He congratulated him on finally, well almost, taking the plunge.

He was a little reluctant at first to talk about Tracey, but alcohol had a tendency to loosen him up. He managed to relate his experience in

Hampton Roads when he returned from Vietnam and that the relationship had basically ended. He added that she had divorced that "guy" and that he met her sometime later with hope. The reunion had been a total disaster--fire and fury. Now he had put dating on the backburner, and he was focused on being successful in the corporate world, specifically with Nation's Automotive Financial Corporation.

He explained the Phoenix Program and the promised managerial career. Morris briefly related his job in the Human Resources department. They never could completely figure out why they had lost touch with each other after Vietnam. They decided to let sleeping dogs lie and be thankful that somehow fate had gotten them back together again.

Dinner was served, and for the first time, Reggie glanced around and took in the full ambiance of the restaurant. It was truly first class. The maître d' welcomed them as they entered the restaurant. The bartender was super, and their waitress was pleasant. He leaned over to Morris and said, "Man, this place is definitely uptown."

They were sitting at a table on the second level overlooking the main dining area. Reggie noticed the elegantly-dressed diners at tables all around him. He commented earlier on Morris's suit. He was thankful that he had worn a sport coat and tie. It wasn't a tuxedo, but he didn't feel too out of place.

While eating and enjoying a nice bottle of wine that Morris had ordered, he glanced down to the main floor dining area and noticed what appeared to be a wedding party of about twenty people eating. The women were all dressed in fancy, long, and flowy gowns. All the men were in black tuxedos with boutonnières in their lapels. There was a couple sitting at the head of the table who were no doubt the bride and groom.

He remembered seeing at least three limos parked outside when he and Morris entered the restaurant. He smiled down at the group who were a little loud, but he thought, *Hey, it's a festive time, so why not let them celebrate?*

He continued to glance down every now and then as he ate and observed the smiling faces and heard the chatter that sounded foreign. He pointed over to Morris and said, "Looks like those guys are having a good time, although I can't make out what nationality they are."

Morris simply shook his head. "Hey, man, up here, in Detroit, we have a lot of ethnic groups. They could be anything."

Reggie nodded and looked down. "I don't know. They sound Russian to me. Anyway, looks like fun down there."

Midway through dinner, as they were clanking their wine glasses and Morris was telling Reggie that he was so glad to see him, they heard a large crash as if something had splintered. They both turned and looked down at the wedding party. They saw a large man grabbing and tossing a smaller man across the table. Glasses, busted plates, flowers, silverware, and lit candles spewed onto the floor. Women started screaming at the wedding party's table and throughout the restaurant. All the men at the table started punching and wrestling with each other. In a split second, the entire wedding party was fighting, including the women. Diners at nearby tables began to get up and run away from the melee as tables and chairs were overturned and thrown.

Reggie and Morris were spellbound for a moment when Reggie exclaimed, "What the . . ."

The second-level diners were now pushing away from their tables, rushing pass Reggie and Morris, and were headed downstairs for the only visible exit. Morris grabbed Reggie's arm and said, "Let's get out of here!"

They, like the other second-level diners, realized that they had to partially pass the fighting party downstairs to make it to the main entrance-exit. Someone yelled out, "He's got a gun!"

The screams in the restaurant got louder as diners were pushing and shoving to make the exit. Morris screamed at Reggie, "Keep moving and stay low!"

With only a couple of chairs landing near them, they managed to squeeze through the exit along with several other diners. As they ran into the parking lot, Morris was about to say, "We made it!" when they heard someone yell, "Freeze!"

"Put your hands behind your heads and get on the ground now!"

Reggie looked in shock as seven police officers pointed their guns at his face.

Morris cried out, "Get down, Reggie. Get down!"

Reggie hesitated.

An officer yelled again, "This is your last warning! On the ground now!"

Morris yelled out again, "Reggie, get down!"

Reggie slowly kneeled and put his hands behind his head. The police officers immediately rushed him and pushed him, along with Morris, to the ground.

Just at that moment, a small, elderly white man in a black tuxedo with a white apron wrapped around him rushed over to the police officers and pleaded. "No, no, officers. These aren't the guys! They have done nothing wrong. The fighters are still in the restaurant."

The police officer who was apparently in charge looked up. "You sure?"

The white elderly man said, "Yes, yes. Please get in there quick."

The policemen stepped over Reggie and Morris and rushed into the restaurant.

Morris breathed a sigh of relief. Reggie rolled over and sat up on the cold asphalt, still fuming inside. He looked over at Morris. "Man, what the hell just happened?"

"Calm down, Reggie, calm down. No harm. It was just a misunderstanding."

"A misunderstanding?"

"Morris, you and I know both know what that was all about. Two black men—"

Morris cut him off. "Yeah, but like I said, we are okay."

He reached down to help Reggie up.

The elderly man came over to them extended his hand to shake and said, "I'm so sorry, gentlemen. I'm the owner, and I sincerely apologize for this unfortunate incident. Please allow me to make it up to you. Your dinner and wine are on the house, and if you ever decide to come back and dine with us again, that dinner too will be on the house." He gave them his card, shook their hands again, and added, "Again, I apologize, but I sincerely hope that I will see you again."

As Reggie and Morris walked back to the car, they could see more officers and large police trucks pulling up. They turned around to look back as police officers were escorting men and women who were hand-cuffed out of the restaurant and putting them in the trucks.

Morris turned to Reggie. "See? Not us."

Reggie looked at him in disgust. "Could have been."

Morris laughed and slapped him on the back. "Hey, look on the bright side, we were racking up north of a 300-dollar dinner tab. Now you still have cash in your wallet and a rain check."

Just as they reached their car, Reggie slightly pushed Morris. "All I got to say is the next time we go out to dinner, I'm picking the restaurant."

CHAPTER 49

It had been a couple of weeks since the restaurant incident, and Reggie had cooled down. He had chalked it up as a thing of the past and just . . . Detroit. In fact, Morris, as he always managed to do, had somehow gotten him to joke about the entire thing. A few days after the incident, Morris invited Reggie over to meet Sheila at their apartment. Sheila seemed to be a nice person and very attractive. On one of the times that she left the room, Reggie whispered to Morris, "Man, you are a fool if you let that woman get away."

Morris just smiled and shook his head but acknowledged to himself that Reggie was right. After hearing Morris relate the restaurant incident, and although it was very serious and scary, Sheila weighed in and was amused. She mentioned to the two that she had read something in the newspapers regarding the incident. She recalled that it apparently was indeed a wedding party. They were a Serbian bride and a Croatian groom. Both sides of the "clans" were doing well until someone allegedly said a disparaging remark about the other's mother country, and all hell broke loose. Reggie added, "Yeah, you can say that again."

They all laughed.

Reggie smiled as he thought about the entire incident as he sat in the small cafeteria waiting for Hector and the rest of the crew to join him for lunch. He was anticipating the ensuing discussion from the group on how they felt about graduation coming up in a few weeks. He knew everyone was excited, but there was still that air of the unknown. What field office were they going to be sent and what was the game plan going forward? No one of authority was saying anything. He had tried several times to pump Greg Morton, but Greg would only smile, pat him on the back, and say, "Not to worry. They are working on it."

He was usually satisfied with Greg's response and felt he could trust what he was saying. Over the past year and a half of the program, he and Greg had gotten close, mainly from Greg prepping him to some degree on what to expect from the Oversee Board Reviews and their many private discussions on corporate politics. He had quickly learned that Greg was a man of his word. If he had a question regarding the program or some phase of the program and Greg didn't know the answer, then he would always get back to him.

He remembered one day in particular from his first few months of the program. It was a Friday evening before a three-day weekend. He had been in the Corral pretty much alone and packing up his things to leave work. Out of the blue, Greg had approached him and asked what his plans were for the weekend. Of course, the first few months of the program had been hell, and he could hardly breathe with Jack Kramer on his back 24/7. Anyway, he had been puzzled by the question but responded that he had nothing to do. He was just going to go home and study or something. Greg had surprised him and said, "Why don't you come out to my place for dinner on Saturday evening? My wife and I would be glad to have you. The weather is supposed to be nice. We can drink a few beers, grill some steaks, and just hang out."

Reggie couldn't help being stunned and couldn't imagine why Greg would extend the offer. He thought to himself that he was probably over thinking things as he sometimes did. He finally said, "Okay."

Greg shook his hand and said, "Good."

He took out a piece of paper and wrote his address and phone number and handed it to Reggie. He then said, "If you have any problems, call me. Otherwise, I will see you on Saturday at six-thirty."

Reggie arrived on time with a bottle of wine and met Greg's lovely and very personable wife, Jackie. They put down more than a few beers, shot a couple games of pool, grilled, had a wonderful steak dinner, and talked a lot about the program. It was an enjoyable evening. He found that Greg was truly a down-to-earth person and genuine. He had asked Reggie out to his home because he felt that he needed a break from the program's grind and the relentlessness of Jack Kramer. Reggie didn't leave until well after midnight, and he left feeling that a personal bond had been created between the two. So much so that he felt comfortable asking Greg anything about the program or the corporation.

He looked at his watch and noted that it had already been thirty minutes into his one-hour scheduled lunch, and no one had shown up yet. He guessed that the crew had been held up and probably wouldn't make it. It was not uncommon because everyone was under so much pressure. There was never a set time for lunch and to meet. People just showed up whenever they could get free and hope that they could sit and exhale for an hour before they were summoned back to the Corral.

His thoughts wandered back, and he was about to gather his lunch tray and return to the Corral when he looked up and saw Roger Hempfell and two of his boys approaching the table.

"Hey, Saunders. Can we join you?"

Reggie rolled his eyes and replied, "I was just leaving," and added, "So what brings you down here?"

Hempfell responded, "Oh, nothing much. Knew you guys hung out down here and just wanted to see how the lower half lives." Hempfell smiled slightly.

Reggie just looked at the three as he stood up.

Hempfell gestured to Reggie. "Hold on, wait a minute. I was just about to congratulate you and your fellow trainees"— he emphasized trainees —"On your upcoming graduation. Heard you were finally getting out of here."

Reggie looked at him, wondering where this was going.

Hempfell continued, "As a matter of fact, we have a little proposition for you." A sly grin was apparent on Hempfell's face. "You see, a little birdie informed us that you, Saunders, played baseball back from . . . Where did you come from?"

Reggie quickly said, "It doesn't matter where I came from. What's your point, Roger?"

"Well, it just so happens that we are in this baseball league, and our team is in first place with the championship game coming up soon. Me and my guys need a little practice before the big game. So we were wondering whether you and your guys would be interested in a friendly game . . . sort of a tune-up for us, and you can look at it as a going away present from us to you."

Reggie stared at Hempfell and said, "You got to be joking, right?"

Hempfell hunched his shoulders and turned to the other two. "Am I joking, guys?"

They all laughed.

"Of course, Saunders, if you aren't up for the challenge and want to punk out on us, it's understandable. I guess once an underdog, always an underdog."

Reggie was boiling inside and thinking to himself, *Man, this stuff is never going to end.* Then he just blurted out, "Okay, Roger, you are on. When and where?"

CHAPTER 50

Back at his workstation in the Corral, Reggie sat silently with his head in his hands. *What was I thinking?* he thought. He had done a good job thus far in mastering the art of not letting Hempfell get to him, and now there was this baseball game that he didn't know how he was going to get out of.

His dilemma and thoughts were interrupted when Hector Perez walked by and said, "Hey, Reggie, I see you are back from lunch. Sorry, I didn't make it, but you know . . . " Hector looked at Reggie and paused. "Hey, man. What's up? You look like you have just been to a funeral."

Reggie slowly looked up. "Hey, Hector."

He paused and thought to himself, *What the heck! Might as well get it out there.* "Hey, man. I need a big favor from you."

Hector looked at him and said, "Hey, no problem. What, man?"

"Well, I have to ask: have you ever played baseball?"

Hector was somewhat surprised and had to think about the question, but he replied, "Yeah, well, if you count stickball in the streets that I used to play back when I was in grade school." He shrugged his shoulders and added, "That's about it."

Reggie thought about Hector's response, shook his head, and said, "Good enough."

Before Hector could ask what was going on, Reggie said, "Hey, Hector, round up all the guys and tell them we are going to meet at Jake's Bar right after work. The beer is on me and tell them it's an emergency."

Hector had no idea where this was going, but he could see that Reggie was excited. He was about to ask again whether or not he was alright, but just then, Roger Hempfell walked into the Corral. Reggie eyed the group entering, gestured to Hector, and quietly said, "Just get everybody there."

Hector understood and responded, "Yeah, okay, man."

Reggie turned around in his workstation and picked up the phone. He had to make two calls.

CHAPTER 51

Later that evening, Reggie, Hector, Sam, Jason, and the rest of the guys sat at small tables in the back of Jake's Bar. Reggie had gotten there earlier and had asked Jake, the owner, if he could cordon off the area in the back of the bar. Jake had said okay, so there they were.

He had already explained the challenge, as he labeled it, to play a baseball game. As he expected, there were many questions. The main question was how were they going to play a baseball game against Hempfell and his boys? Reggie apologized and repeatedly told the group that he probably should have just kept his big mouth shut and let it pass, and now he was thinking he might as well go to Hempfell and call the game off.

After hearing Reggie apologize several times, Hector looked around at the group, stood up, and said, "No, man, you did the right thing." He addressed the other men. "Hempfell and his boys have been dogging us all the time that we have been up here. We have been their whipping boys. I've been wanting to go up and punch that bastard, but countless times," now he pointed to Reggie, "Reggie, you have reeled me in and said let it be, take the high road, and turn the other cheek."

He smiled looking at Reggie. "Yeah, all that Golden Rule stuff. But it worked, man. We have all weathered the storm, and we are getting the hell out of Dodge in a few weeks. So I don't know how we are going to do it, but I'd rather go down fighting than to see that smirk on Hempfell's face. I know our chances are slim to none. Anyway . . . " He looked at Reggie. "I'm sorry, man, but he just might get an errant baseball thrown to the back of his head."

Everyone laughed, and then there was a quiet calm as reality set in.

Jason finally broke the silence and said what was obviously on the group's mind, "But how are we going do it? Those guys are good."

Reggie immediately jumped back in, pointed toward the entrance of the bar, and said, "With a little practice and with the help of that guy walking toward us now."

Morris Whitehead approached the tables, and Reggie immediately made the introduction. "Gentlemen, meet my best friend and baseball infielder extraordinaire, Morris Whitehead."

Morris smiled and shook hands with the group while saying, "I wouldn't go so far as to say all that, but when I got the call from Reggie, well, he made me an offer I couldn't refuse. It was a no-brainer. I'm in."

Reggie had to smile remembering the phone call and conversation he had earlier with Morris. It was a wild shot, but before Morris could object, he had thrown in a little reminder. "Hey, dude, you owe me one from that restaurant fiasco."

Morris had had to laugh, but reluctantly agreed that he had to even the score. He looked at the assembled group now, turned to Reggie, and said, "What's the plan?"

CHAPTER 52

With a couple of long practices under their belts, Reggie was walking along the first base side of the makeshift practice field at the back of an abandoned warehouse just outside of the city. He was looking toward what was carved out as an outfield: lots of dirt, gravel, and very little grass. He was watching Morris hit fly balls to the designated outfielders. As most of the balls were hitting the ground and not being caught, he shook his head and thought to himself, *Man, this doesn't look good.*

He walked a little further down the right side of the field to the potato sack filled with sand that was first base, kicked it slightly to realign it, and sighed. *Well, it is what it is.*

He looked back out to the outfield and saw Morris coming toward him.

"Hey, Reggie, not too promising, but we have one more practice before the game. And, hey, man, we just have to make it work." He patted Reggie on the shoulder and added, "However, I do see one major flaw in your fielding assignments. I think you have everyone in the position that will be best for the team." He crossed his fingers. "But what about a catcher? I mean, I can play any position, but if you want me at shortstop." He raised his hands. "I know I'm good, but I can't play all nine positions at once."

He shook his head and added, "And Jason, I know you like him at that spot, but he knows nothing about being a catcher."

Reggie held his head down, shuffled his feet in the dirt, lightly kicked the potato sack again, and said, "Yeah, I know, but I got one more ace up my sleeve."

Morris looked at him and asked, "Oh, really?"

"Yeah, I just got confirmation earlier this morning. An old classmate of mine who just happens to be a hell of a catcher has family here in Detroit. Well, not really his family, but his wife's. Anyway, as a huge favor to me, he's convinced his wife to visit her family, and he's agreed to play. There's only one condition though."

Morris was still listening intently.

"He can only play the day of the game. In other words, he will show up at game time."

Morris stepped back and said, "Whoa, man. You are joking, right?"

Reggie shook his head, smiling, and said, "No, man. I'm dead serious."

Morris added, "This guy must be good."

Reggie continued, "Mac. Yeah, Mac is the best. He and I played in community college out in California. He caught all the games that I pitched. He knows me like a book. I'm convinced that between you at shortstop, me pitching, and Mac catching, we might just have a chance."

Morris thought for a moment and finally said, "That reminds me, when was the last time you actually pitched in a baseball game?"

Reggie had to think about the question and was no way going to respond to it because he knew it was too long ago. He simply reversed his response and said, "When was the last time you played shortstop?"

Morris looked at Reggie, laughed, punched him lightly in the shoulder, and said, "Man, you are insane, but let's do this!"

CHAPTER 53

Mother Nature had cooperated as far as the weather was concerned with bright blue skies and lots of sunshine. It was a perfect day for baseball with temperatures in the seventies. Not bad and unexpected for Detroit weather, even though it was June. Usually, one could still expect cold and dreary weather.

Even better was the ball field. They all had to admit that the field was immaculate. It was definitely set up professionally; there was manicured grass in the outfield, and the infield was graded out with smooth dirt. The baselines and outfield lines were all chalked out in white. The entire outfield was fenced in and had large white markings designating the home-run distances. There were opposite side dugouts for the home team and visiting team plus bleachers for the fans.

As Reggie and the others were getting their gear out of the cars and walking toward the field, Roger Hempfell and a couple of his guys walked over.

"Hey, Saunders. I must admit we didn't think you guys would show up." He looked toward the skies, smirked, and added, "Great day for an ass-kicking."

Reggie didn't take the bait and simply responded, "We'll see, Roger. We'll see."

Hempfell stared at him and the others and looked as if he were going to say something else, but just then, an older gentleman approached the group. Hempfell abruptly turned and rejoined the rest of his team who were warming up on the playing field.

The older gentleman was dressed in black and was obviously the umpire. He acknowledged Reggie and his group and then said, "Welcome, gentlemen. I along with," he looked back toward the field and pointed to two other men, "will be umpiring the game today. You will be the visiting team, and your dugout is over there along the first-base side." He looked at his watch. "You will have about thirty minutes to take the field and warm up. The All-Stars will be finishing up in a moment."

Reggie and the others looked out over the field as they saw Hempfell and his guys slowly coming off the field from their warm up. They were all dressed in matching uniforms. He looked at himself and his guys dressed in various colors of T-shirts, long pants, short pants, and different colored baseball caps. They were lucky to have gloves, a few balls, and a couple of bats, much less uniforms. They were definitely ragtag compared to Hempfell's bunch, and he could feel that his guys were a little intimidated.

The umpire had just finished up with the rules. He asked Reggie for his lineup sheet. Reggie had taken great pains the night before to come up with something. When he thought about it more, it hadn't been too hard because the bottom line was that he only had nine guys, plus Morris and Mac, if he showed up. It was just a matter of putting a name down beside a position.

The umpire took his sheet, glanced at it for a moment, and then said, "Okay, the only thing I will need is the name of your team."

After all his deliberation the night before, Reggie hadn't thought about a name for the team. He looked at the umpire and glanced back at the group. No one said anything. Morris just hunched his shoulders.

The umpire added, "We have the All-Stars over there. I mean, this is just a pickup game. I can leave it blank."

Reggie said, "No."

He paused, took the sheet back from the umpire, and wrote a name down. The umpire took the sheet back, looked at it, and said, "Okay, Team Phoenix it is. Gentlemen, you can take the field. You have thirty minutes."

CHAPTER 54

Morris hurriedly walked over to Reggie. "Hey, man. Our time is just about up. Where is our catcher?"

Reggie looked at his watch and glanced toward the parking lot. "He said he would be here."

Just then, he saw a stocky, sandy-haired man carrying catcher gear walking toward them. He quickly walked over to greet Mac and help him with his gear. Mac dropped everything, and they embraced.

"Mac, thanks so much for coming. Man, you look great."

Mac was equally happy and replied, "No problem, Saunders. It took a few deep conversations with my wife, but man, I wouldn't miss this for the world. Sorry, I'm late, but I took a wrong turn and had to do a little backtracking. By the way, you look great, too. How's the old pitching arm?"

Before Reggie could respond, Morris walked up behind them and grunted. Reggie spun around and said, "Pardon my manners. This is also an old friend. Mac, meet Morris."

They shook hands, and Morris pointed to his watch. "You guys have about five minutes to warm up."

Mac said, "I'm good, Reggie, but why don't you throw me a few balls so that I can gauge what you got?"

He added, "By the way, who are we playing, and how did this game all come about?"

Reggie looked at him. "It's a long story, Mac, but let's get in a few pitches, get our signals coordinated, and I will introduce you to the rest of our team. Maybe someday, way into the future, I'll explain."

Mac looked at him and laughed. "Some things never change, do they?"

Five minutes later, the umpire yelled out, "Play ball!"

Hempfell and the All-Stars took to the field. It was no surprise to see that Roger was the pitcher for his team. What was a surprise, as Reggie and Team Phoenix would find out later, was that he was very good at it.

CHAPTER 55

It was the top of the sixth inning now, and thus far, Reggie and everyone else on the team except Morris had not gotten a solid hit off Hempfell. There were a couple of walks, but in every case, no one could advance the runners. Reggie had struck out twice, Mac once, and the others . . . Well, it didn't look good. Still, they were in the game because somehow he had willed himself up to the challenge. With Mac directing his pitches, they had been relatively successful in keeping the All-Stars in check. There were several scattered hits and more than a few errors by Team Phoenix up to this point, but the score was a respectable two to zero in favor of the All-Stars.

Jason had just struck out to end the inning, and Team Phoenix was taking the field. Mac walked up to the mound to talk to Reggie. "You are doing good, man. They are only up two. We will eventually get to this guy. Meanwhile, you just keep throwing the off-speed stuff. I can tell that they are not used to seeing junk, and man, you got it today."

Reggie said, "Yeah, right now I don't trust my fastball. I mean, I think I still can put a little heat on it, but—"

Mac interrupted him. "How is the old arm?"

Reggie shook his head and said, "Feels like it's going to drop off."

Mac responded, "I got a jar of heat in my bag. We'll rub it down after this inning. Right now, just hang in there with the slow stuff."

They could hear the umpire say, "Play ball."

Mac went back behind the plate.

At that same moment, one of Roger Hempfell's guys, Todd Albertson, walked over to him in the dugout.

"Man, I have to admit Saunders is better than we ever imagined. So far, it's been pop-ups, ground balls, long fly balls, and strikeouts. He's caught me looking twice."

Hempfell looked up and replied, "Yeah, but don't be a whiner. We can get to him. He's about gassed now. We are up two to zip. Let's close this thing out."

Albertson walked away and sat down at the other end of the bench. He was going to say to Hempfell, "Yeah, but we are up only two runs because of their outfield errors. If you take them away, the score would be zero to zero," but he thought better of it. He put his head down and hoped that the game would soon be over.

Reggie got lucky in the bottom of the sixth inning. He was able to get the first batter at the bottom of the All-Stars lineup to pop up behind the plate. Mac made the catch for an out. The second batter hit a slow grounder back to him, which he easily threw the runner out at first base. The third batter sharply hit a ball to shortstop that Morris swooped down on with a backhand grab and fired to first base to end the inning.

At the top of the seventh inning with two outs, things changed. A break happened. Reggie was up at bat and took Hempfell to a three and two count. Hempfell's next pitch was a called ball by the umpire. He was furious with the call and gestured toward the umpire. His catcher, shortstop, and second baseman rushed to the mound to calm him down and prevent him from being thrown out of the game. Of course, this was all to Reggie's delight as he raced down the first baseline to step on the bag. Team Phoenix's bench was beginning to stir. Morris rushed over to first base, and from the coaches' circle, he leaned over and whispered in Reggie's ear, "You up for stealing a base?"

Reggie looked at him, smiled, and said, "Watch me."

Two pitches later, he was racing down the base path to second. With a hair-late throw and a great slide, he was called safe. Team Phoenix players were getting a little excited for the first time in the game.

Mac was up next and also managed to work Hempfell and finally drew a walk. He trotted down to first base. There was a big powwow on the mound as Hempfell was visibly pissed off. The second baseman, shortstop, and catcher were talking to him.

The shortstop said, "Hey, settle down, Roger. We got this, but I think we should walk this next batter."

Hempfell looked over to Team Phoenix's side of the field and saw Morris standing in the batters' circle, swinging a couple of bats.

The second baseman said, "Yeah, I agree, and I know it would be loading the bases, but this guy has hit you hard his last two times at bat."

The catcher chimed in, "No sense in going down that road. If we put him on, the next batter is a piece of cake. You can mow him down, man . . . You got this."

They all nodded their heads in agreement, but Hempfell said, "No way, man. No way am I intentionally walking this guy. No way I do three walks in a row. I'm pitching to him, and he's going down."

The catcher looked at the two other guys, back at Hempfell, and then simply said, "Okay, but just keep things down and away from this guy."

Hempfell shrugged his shoulders as the umpire said, "Let's go, guys. Play ball."

With Reggie at second base and Mac at first, Morris dug in at the plate and waited with no intent to swing at the first pitch. He guessed right as Hempfell's throw was up high and inside. The catcher walked halfway to the mound and made a gesture to his pitcher and said, "Take a deep breath, slow it down and keep it low."

Morris took the opportunity to step out of the batter's box. He took a couple of practice swings as he stared down Hempfell. He knew that he had to continue this mind game that he and Hempfell had been playing. He smiled as he stepped back to the plate, thinking that all he wanted was his pitch. His prayer was answered. The second pitch was a fastball right down the middle just above the waist. With a powerful swing, the ball went soaring over the center field fence . . . Homerun!

Team Phoenix went crazy as Reggie and Mac waited at the plate as Morris trotted around the bases and touched home plate. The score was now three to two in favor of Team Phoenix. Hempfell held his head down and looked over at the All-Stars dugout. His catcher walked up to the mound and gave him a new ball and said, "We got our work cut out for us. Let's get this next batter, and then we go to work on Saunders."

The score didn't change as Reggie and Team Phoenix were able to hold the All-Stars scoreless at the bottom of the seventh inning and the bottom of the eighth inning.

CHAPTER 56

With the score still three to two in favor of Team Phoenix, Reggie, Mac, and Morris found themselves in the bottom of the ninth inning with the meat of the All-Stars lineup due to bat.

They were standing on the mound as Mac again said to Reggie, "How's the arm?"

Reggie rubbed his right arm with his left hand and replied, "Burning like hell. The 'heat' is really heating it up."

Morris added, "Well this is it, homeboy. I think it's up to us to finish this thing and go home."

Mac gave Reggie the ball and added, "Yeah, just keep it slow and low. You've had them off-balance all day. They haven't figured you out yet. Just keep them hitting pop-ups and ground balls to the shortstop."

He smiled as he slapped Morris on the shoulder. Reggie nodded his head in agreement, rolled the ball in his glove a couple of times, and said, "Okay, let's end this thing now."

Team Phoenix found that ending the game was easier said than done. Reggie struck out the first batter, but the next batter managed to get a base hit through the infield on the second-base side. The runner then advanced to second base on a wild pitch from him. Mac had blocked the pitch and didn't let the ball get by him, but he was unable to make the throw to second base. Reggie was obviously tiring and subsequently walked the next batter who trotted down to first base. With only one out and runners at first and second base, Mac walked halfway up to the mound and pointed to the ground to signal to Reggie to keep the ball low.

The next batter took Reggie to three balls and two strikes. He hit the next pitch, a high pop-up to center field. Hector Perez was running around the outfield in circles, seemingly trying to zero in on the ball. To Team Phoenix's relief, he made the catch for the second out. However, the runners were able to tag up and advance to second and third base before Hector's throw back to the infield.

With two outs in the books, Mac, Reggie, and Morris were on the mound again trying to decide what they should do to preserve the win. Morris spoke first. "I don't know, man. This next guy can hit, and then we got Hempfell on deck. He can hit."

Mac joined in, "Yeah, it comes down to the lesser of two evils."

They both looked at Reggie as Mac handed him the ball.

"Your call."

Reggie didn't hesitate. "We intentionally walk the next batter, and then it's me facing Hempfell."

He smiled. "Hey, you can't ask for a better ending one way or another. This was meant to be."

Mac looked at Morris and turned and walked back to home plate. Morris slapped Reggie on the back and said, "Go get him, Silk."

Mac was now positioning himself behind the plate. He assumed a half-squatting stance with his catcher's mitt hovering just outside the corner of the plate. Reggie nodded in agreement and wound up for his first pitch, a called ball by the umpire. Hempfell was standing in the batters on deck circle. He and the rest of the All-Stars now knew what was happening: an intentional walk with Hempfell due next at the plate.

Three wide outside pitches later, the batter was trotting down to first to load the bases. Hempfell knocked his bat against his cleats and then stepped to the plate.

Mac stood up, took a couple of steps in front of the plate, pointed to Reggie, and tossed the ball back. Reggie caught the ball and slapped it three times in his glove while he momentarily paced around the mound. He stopped and then stared directly down at home plate. Hempfell smiled and pointed his bat toward the outfield.

Everyone knew he was telling Reggie that the ball was going over the fence. The tension could be felt by both dugouts as everyone stood up knowing that this was the ball game, one way or another.

Reggie's arm was still burning and felt like it would be severed from his body, but he knew he had to somehow find the strength to deliver hopefully four or five more pitches. He took the sign from Mac and his first pitch was a little high and wide for a called ball. Hempfell stepped away from the plate, took a couple of practice swings, and stepped back. Reggie took the sign from Mac and delivered an inside slow curveball. Hempfell came around with his swing, and there was a loud cracking sound as the ball jumped off his bat and headed for deep left field. However, it was hooking and just went left of the foul line. There was a noticeable gasp from Team Phoenix as everyone in the dugout exhaled.

Mac stood up again and walked a couple of steps toward Reggie, who stepped off the mound, taking a couple of steps to hear him.

"It's okay. No harm. Just keep it low."

With his arm throbbing, Reggie knew he was losing control, but he had to *will* himself to deliver the ball where Mac wanted it thrown. His next pitch didn't go as low as he had hoped, but fortunately, Hempfell swung ahead of the pitch and foul-tipped it back behind the plate for a strike.

The count was now one ball and two strikes. Reggie took a deep breath. His next pitch could be it. He wound up and threw, but the ball was too low and hit the dirt in front of the plate. Mac managed to block it and kept it in front of him. The runner at third base started to run down the baseline to possibly score, but Mac quickly pounced on the ball and threw it to third base just a tad late to get the runner, who had made a beeline back to the bag. The count now stood at two balls and two strikes.

Reggie stepped off the mound and picked up his rosin bag. He twisted it in his hand, hoping that it would give him a tighter grip on the ball. He wiped his hands on his pants. Hempfell took the opportunity to step away from the plate. They both stared at each other. The mind game was continuing. Hempfell took his time, but when the umpire looked at him, he got the message and stepped back to the plate.

Reggie took the sign from Mac, wound up, and threw what both he and Mac thought was a strike on the inside corner. However, the umpire differed, and it was a called ball. Again, Hempfell smiled and stepped away from the plate.

CHAPTER 57

With the count at three balls and two strikes, Mac motioned to the umpire for a time out and approached Reggie on the mound. Morris ran over to join the summit. Mac partially raised his catcher's mask from his face and said, "Well, gentlemen, here we are." He then added, "Have you got one more pitch in you, Saunders?"

Morris slapped Reggie on the back and answered the question, "Yeah, he's got one more pitch. Right, Silk?"

Reggie responded, "Yeah, it's now or never."

Mac jumped back in, "Okay, but let's go with the slow curveball low and inside. He can't afford to take a chance that it could be called a ball. He'll swing and hopefully won't make solid contact. We can hope for a ground ball or short pop-up."

Reggie nodded, saying, "Okay."

The umpire walked halfway up to the group and said, "Alright, gentlemen; let's play ball."

Mac slapped the ball into Reggie's glove and said, "It's all on you, Silk."

He went back to home plate and knelt as Hempfell stepped back into the batter's box. He gave Reggie the sign for the slow and low inside curveball.

To his amazement and shock, Reggie shook off the sign. Mac thought to himself, *What?*

He gave Reggie the sign again. Reggie shook his head. "No."

Mac, still confused and in disbelief, shifted and thought, *Okay, let's try another. How about slow, low, and away?*

Again, Reggie shook his head. "No."

Now Mac was really getting concerned. He stood up behind the plate and looked at Reggie as if to say, "What are you doing?"

Reggie motioned Mac to get back behind the plate. Mac was still shaking his head and thinking, *Well, there's only one pitch left.* He gave the sign. This time Reggie nodded his head.

Meanwhile, Hempfell was salivating and saying to himself, *Gotcha now. I know you are coming with that slow curveball. This time it won't be a foul ball. It's going over the fence.* He dug his cleats deeper in at the plate.

It seemed like forever as Mac waited for the pitch. He was still thinking in fast time, *What is he thinking? It's got to be years since he's thrown that pitch.*

Morris, on the other hand, could see the back and forth with the signals between the two. He knew what was happening. He had witnessed it several years ago in a baseball game in Vietnam. This was Silk on the mound. He looked up at the sky, hoping that the next pitch was the one: Silk's patented fastball.

Reggie took a deep breath and summoned what little strength he had left. He wound up. Hempfell was eyeing the movement, tightened the grip on his bat, and said to himself, *Here it comes.*

Reggie threw the fastball to Mac's dismay right down the middle of the plate waist-high. He shifted, followed the pitch, and saw Hempfell wind his bat and take a mighty swing.

Everything seemed to continue in slow motion. Then the ball just zipped into Mac's mitt with a loud popping sound. Hempfell's bat was wrapped around his body. Swing and a miss!

The umpire yelled an emphatic, "Strike three!"

Then everything went crazy. Team Phoenix ran out of the dugout and raced to the mound ahead of Mac and Morris. The infield and outfield rushed in, and in a manner of seconds, the entire team was on top of each other, celebrating and congratulating Reggie, who was on the bottom of the human pile. No one could actually believe what had just happened. Hempfell walked dejectedly back to his dugout, tossing his batter's helmet to the ground.

The euphoria seemed to last forever. No one wanted to leave the field, but finally, someone yelled out, "Party at Jake's!"

Everyone continued to slap each other as they started gathering their gear. Reggie added to the excitement by shouting out, "Beer's on me!"

Mac walked up to Reggie and asked, "How's the arm feeling, old man?"

Reggie quickly responded, "Don't touch it. It might fall off."

They both laughed. Mac added, "Wish I could join you for the celebration, but I told the wife that I would leave as soon as the game was over."

Reggie embraced Mac.

"Thanks so much, Mac. We couldn't have done it without you. I understand, and please tell Judy thanks for allowing me to borrow you. I have your address and phone number, and I promise to keep in touch. Although I have to be honest with you, the likelihood of me ever being in the state of Idaho is virtually zero. Hey, but I plan to stay in touch."

Mac nodded and said, "Okay, man. I have your information and who knows? Never say never. We might meet up again. Heck, I still have one or two more baseball games left in me."

They both laughed and shook hands.

Mac walked away, finally saying, "See you, Saunders."

Reggie walked to the dugout to gather his gear, looked up, and saw Todd Albertson from the All-Stars coming his way. As Albertson approached, he extended his hand out to Reggie.

"Congratulations, Saunders."

Reggie was a little taken aback, but he shook his hand, saying, "Thanks."

Albertson was one of the MBAs at headquarters and the Corral, and up until now, he had not really communicated with Reggie in any meaningful way. He was also one of Hempfell's main crew members. Reggie glanced over in the direction of the All-Stars dugout and could see only a couple of guys left packing their things. He looked at Albertson and wondered what it was all about.

Albertson smiled and added, "One heck of a game. Never would have believed that you and your guys could pull it off." He looked Reggie in the eye. "Anyway, just wanted to say that there are some guys in the Corral pulling for you guys and are happy that you all are going to graduate and be placed out into field offices."

Reggie stepped back a little.

"Well, let me guess: Hempfell isn't one of those guys."

Albertson replied, "Roger, well you just have to live with Roger. He will be mad as hell for a while, but hey, he will eventually get over it . . . Well, maybe."

They both laughed.

Reggie still felt a little awkward but managed to say, "Hey, man, thanks for the congrats, and by the way, I hope you guys do well in the championship game next week."

Albertson shook his head. "Well, if we don't run into a pitcher like you, we just might have a chance."

He patted Reggie on his left shoulder and shook his hand again. "See you in the Corral on Monday."

CHAPTER 58

THE PHOENIX PROGRAM

Chris Roden sat stoically as Daniel Hartsdale paced around his desk. Roden watched him finally sit down. He was wondering why he had been summoned to the early morning meeting by Hartsdale. Hartsdale had a grim look on his face. He spoke, "Chris, as you know, there was a board meeting and vote last night. The news is already all over the building. Curtis Livingston, our esteemed president of the corporation and chairman of the board, has stepped down due to medical issues. It was a secret, but a few knew that he had suffered a heart attack while playing golf. Due to the resulting complications, he's not coming back. So the board acted swiftly and drafted a letter of retirement."

Hartsdale paused before continuing. "The meeting went back and forth with all the members having something to say as to what direction the corporation should go and, of course, and who to elect as a new leader. Without Livingston's support, I was facing a shit storm."

Roden shifted in his chair.

Hartsdale continued, "Brenner finally had the opportunity he had hoped for. He manipulated enough support to swing the vote." Hartsdale leaned back in his chair and sighed.

"Bottom line, I'm out, and he will soon be in."

Roden hung his head low upon hearing the news.

Hartsdale added, "Also, they terminated the Phoenix Program. I know you were beginning to work on a possible second group coming up to headquarters, but Brenner has made sure that's not going to happen."

Hartsdale leaned forward. "I guess there is a silver lining in all this. I was able to get them to assure me that everyone in the existing program would graduate and be assigned to a field office as a manager."

Roden nodded and said, "Is there anything I can do, Dan?"

"No, Chris, you know how this works. As I said, the program is dead, but you and your staff did a heck of a job getting those young men ready. As I told the board, I have no doubt that the program was a success and was what the corporation needed to do and now."

Hartsdale looked around his office. "Anyway, I guess I'll be packing some boxes." He took a deep breath. "So thanks for everything, Chris. The other news is that I made sure as a quid-pro-quo before I stepped down that you and your staff would be free to resume normal work activities here in headquarters."

Roden wanted to say something, anything, but just couldn't find the words. Hartsdale picked up on his despair.

"Don't worry about me, Chris. I will be okay. My attorney is already negotiating a financial exit for me. I have a number of options, and I will find a way to make it work. I think when all the dust clears, I will still be in the area."

There was a brief moment of silence before Hartsdale finally said, "Chris, there is just one more thing, and I think since he is close to the situation, you had better let Greg Morton handle it."

CHAPTER 59

Reggie sat quietly at his workstation in the Corral. The euphoria of the baseball game had finally subsided and had given way to the new excitement of everyone finding out where their field assignments would be. Sam, Jason, Hector, along with several others, had gotten their assignments. They had sent Sam to Japan. Jason was sent to Boston, and Hector was going to Arizona. All had boxed up their things, said goodbye to Reggie, and were on their way home for a two-week vacation before reporting to their field office assignments. There were only a few guys left, plus Reggie, who were wondering why they hadn't heard anything yet.

There was a calm in the Corral. Roger Hempfell, who had been pretty quiet since the game, and his cronies were away down in Florida (Disney World) for a leadership conference. Reggie's thoughts were interrupted as Greg Morton walked into the room.

"Hey, Reggie, have you got a moment?"

Reggie flipped his pen on his desk, anticipating some good news. "Yeah, sure, Greg. What's up?"

Greg motioned to the door. "Why don't you follow me?"

Reggie got up and followed him down a few corridors of the building. He noticed that they were doing a lot of walking down back corridors. He finally asked, "Greg, where are we going?"

Morton replied, "It's okay, only a little further," as they approached an elevator.

Morton was still quiet as he punched a button, and they waited for the familiar ding of the doors opening. Reggie stepped in and looked at the quilted-lined walls. It was most definitely a freight elevator. Morton remained silent and pushed the button for the thirty-seventh floor.

A moment later, they stepped out into a semi-darkened hallway and began to walk toward a partially-opened door. As they approached, Morton said, "We are here."

He gently tapped on the door while opening it fully and said to the occupant, "He's here, sir."

He motioned Reggie in.

A tall, slightly-graying man stood up from behind a brown metal desk with his hand extended. "Hello, Reginald. It's good to finally meet you."

Reggie was shell-shocked and in awe because he realized he was shaking the hand of Mr. Daniel Hartsdale, executive vice president of operations. He was basically speechless but managed to utter, "Good to meet you, sir."

Greg Morton quietly stepped out of the room, closing the door.

Hartsdale immediately gestured to Reggie to sit down. He was pointing to a rather worn out folding chair in front of the metal desk. He quickly sat while wondering what in the world was happening. He looked around the small room that was basically a closet of some sort. It had shelves and boxes lined up in a corner. The only thing on the desk was a phone. He could also see a briefcase on the floor that was leaning against the desk. He thought to himself, *Man, this is weird. This is the executive vice president, and he's in this closet?*

Hartsdale went around and sat behind the desk. He smiled, spread his arms, and said, "Welcome to the penthouse."

Reggie could only nod. He didn't know whether the statement was a joke or what. Hartsdale leaned over and said, "I guess you are wondering why you are here."

Reggie nodded.

Hartsdale continued. "Well, I will be quick and to the point." He looked at the door and his watch and added, "I only have a few minutes before they will be up here to escort me out of the building."

Reggie was puzzled by the comment but said nothing because he was still thoroughly confused.

"Reginald." Hartsdale paused. "Do you go by Reginald or . . . "

Reggie interrupted and said, "Reggie, sir."

"Okay, then Reggie it is, and please call me Dan."

Reggie instinctively responded, "Okay, sir."

He immediately recoiled, knowing that it would be difficult to break the habit of respectfully addressing his superiors. Hartsdale ignored the "sir," folded his hands, and continued.

"Here's why I asked to see you. You probably don't know that I'm the creator of the Phoenix Program. It's my brainchild. With the assistance and hard work of a lot of people, especially Chris Roden and Greg Morton, the program was put together. We were successful in getting you and the others up to headquarters to learn how the corporation operates and to prepare you to become managers in the field offices and beyond."

Reggie didn't move a muscle and continued to listen.

Hartsdale seemed to relax a little and added, "That's the good news."

Reggie stirred as Hartsdale cleared his throat.

"The bad news is that due to—let's just say unforeseen circumstances— the program has been shut down."

That statement sent a million thoughts through Reggie's head. None good. First and foremost, was he being told that he would not become a manager and be assigned a field office?

Hartsdale saw the bewildered look on his face and held up his hand to further explain. "But you and the remaining group will still get your assignment to a field office. It's that your group will be 'it' for a while."

Reggie sat back in his chair relieved and thought to himself, *Okay, okay, crushing news, but no harm. I still get my assignment.*

Hartsdale noticed the relief in his face and continued, "So there you have it." Hartsdale paused. "However, there is just one more thing I wanted to run by you."

Reggie's relief was short-lived. *Uh-oh, here comes the bomb.*

"Reggie, you have done quite well in the program. Of course, I anticipated that you would. From the very beginning, when I looked at your personnel file, I could tell that you had the makings of a born leader. Both Chris Roden and Greg Morton have related to me that you will do a fine job in the field and perhaps create an opportunity to go even further in the corporation."

Reggie's heart was pumping like crazy. He could only answer, "Thank you, sir."

The room seemed to be getting really warm now. He was sweating a little. Hartsdale wiped his brow before speaking.

"So here's where I throw you a curveball. I'm going to be leaving the corporation." He looked at his watch again. "As a matter of fact, in a few minutes, I won't have a real job."

Reggie just stared. He couldn't believe or understand why Hartsdale was leaving the corporation.

"Anyway, I've made up my mind to take this opportunity to do what I've always wanted to do: start my own company."

Reggie's eyes were as big as melons.

"I know this is sounding crazy to you, but I need good people to assist me in getting it up and running. I wanted to extend to you an opportunity for you to join me. Right now, the accommodations would be nothing like here at headquarters. I will be basically working out of my garage until I get clients, etc."

He looked at Reggie, adding, "I could explain more if you are interested."

He reached into his briefcase and took out a piece of paper, wrote his phone number on it, and handed it to Reggie before adding, "Call me if you are interested. Look, Reggie, there is no pressure here. Like I said, I need good people, and I certainly consider you in that category. Frankly, I know this is coming out of left field, and there are no guarantees. I can't tell you what I would do if the offer were reversed. Right now, you are on your way to possibly the best job and career imaginable. You'll finally get that big office in the back corner of the room. You'll have a great salary, bonuses, company car, and membership at golf country clubs."

He raised his hands and said, "Who could ask for anything more?" He paused. "Anyway, think about it."

Hartsdale once more looked at his watch. He got up and shook Reggie's hand. "Call me if you are interested."

Greg Morton stepped into the room and motioned Reggie out.

Morton was still quiet as they walked down the hallway back to the elevator. Reggie was still in disbelief and trying to process the last ten minutes. Finally, he asked Morton, "Man, did you know anything about what just happened?"

Morton smiled and replied, "I told you it would be okay, and by the way, I have your field office assignment."

Reggie was once more excited. "Don't hold back on me, Greg. Where am I going?"

As they approached the elevator, Reggie couldn't contain himself. "I bet it's Atlanta, right?"

"Just calm down. No, it's not Atlanta, although that would be ideal for you."

He turned to Reggie. "No, we aren't going to send any of you guys down South. We want to make sure you have a reasonable chance to succeed. We are making progress down there, but the culture and attitudes are hard to change. We still have our work cut out for us."

Reggie immediately understood.

"So, my good friend, we are keeping you up North and East."

The elevator doors opened, and two security guards stepped out and headed down the hallway. Morton stepped in with Reggie and pushed the button to close the doors. As they descended, Morton slapped Reggie on the shoulder and said, "You are going to love your assignment. I'm going to miss you. Stay in touch."

CHAPTER 60

ROSSLYN, VIRGINIA

Reggie continued to stare out the window thinking, *Greatest phone call I ever made*, the call that had changed his life. It was a tough and risky decision, but now thinking back, it could not have worked out better. He had stayed in Detroit long enough to finish his college courses and get his four-year degree. Now he was back home in D.C. and a vice president of an up-and-coming finance company. He was still thinking to himself, *Man, it's been one hell of a ride. What's it been? Two years?*

As he continued his thoughts, a meteorite streaked across the night sky. He watched it disappear behind the Jefferson Memorial and hoped that it meant continued good luck. He took a deep breath as he was finishing his thoughts, *And the rest . . . Well, the rest is . . .*

"Mr. Saunders? Mr. Saunders?"

Reggie turned from the window.

"Mr. Saunders, I'm sorry to disturb you."

It was Clara, his secretary. "But I wanted to tell you that I'm leaving for the evening."

Reggie shook his head and responded, "Oh, hi, Clara. Sorry, I didn't hear you come in. Hey, yeah, get out of here and enjoy your weekend. As a matter of fact, I'm getting out of here too. I will take the elevator down with you."

Clara smiled and added, "Oh, I also wanted to tell you that your airline tickets for Detroit are in so you are all set to go."

Reggie said, "Thanks."

While Clara watched him gather his things, she said, "I hear Detroit is nice this time of year, and it's so nice to travel for something fun like a wedding."

He was turning the lights off and heading for the door. "Yeah, it's been a while since I was there, but I plan on having fun seeing an old friend and doing my due diligence as best man."

CHAPTER 61

DETROIT, MICHIGAN

"**H**urry up, man. We are late for the rehearsal dinner."

Reggie was looking at his watch and standing in the living room of Morris's apartment. Morris stepped out of the bathroom, walking a little sluggishly and still adjusting his clothes.

"Don't worry, my best man. All I need is to take a couple of aspirin, and I will be okay."

He added, "No thanks to you. By the way, what time did you drop me off after the bachelor party last night?" He shook his head, "Or was it this morning?"

Reggie laughed and said, "Let's just say that neither one of us has gotten more than a few hours of sleep. I see now why Sheila decided to leave early and leave me with the job of getting you up and out of here. I hope the cold shower did the trick for you."

Morris walked slowly to his kitchen and got a glass of water before taking the aspirin. Then he said, "Let's go."

On the drive over to the rehearsal dinner, Reggie was thinking to himself that he had never been to a wedding rehearsal dinner before. He didn't know exactly what he was supposed to do. So he asked Morris what happened and how it worked. Morris had a perplexed look on his face as he responded, "Hey, man, I'm not really sure. I guess they vary from wedding to wedding, but Sheila is handling everything. So I'm just following her lead."

As he was answering and to Reggie's dismay, Morris drove through a yellow light before continuing,

"But if I had to really guess, I'd say she will have her maid of honor there and of course you and me. There will probably be her parents, my parents, the other bridesmaids, my other groomsmen to match up with the maids, and the minister."

Reggie continued to listen to Morris with great interest.

"I guess we will just walk through everything and then sit down, make some small talk, and eat."

Reggie asked, "Small talk?"

"Yeah, you know, just friendly chatter with the bridesmaids."

"But I don't know any of them."

"Hey, man, I don't really know any of them either. I've seen pictures of some of them, but they are Sheila's sorority sisters coming into Detroit from all over. Hey, I don't know. . . just talk." Morris glanced over and could see that Reggie was uneasy.

He smiled. "Hey, when in doubt, just use the old 'Silk' line."

Reggie shook his head slowly. "No, man. I don't know. My Silk days may be numbered. I mean, I'm still having fun and all, but sometimes things or relationships just begin to get shallow and end up nowhere and—"

Morris humorlessly interjected, "Really, are we getting bored now? I seem to remember if we go way back in history that I was the one who gave you the Silk name. However, since we are on the subject, I noticed something on the picture that you sent me of your Corvette, and I've been meaning to ask you. I mean, I get the Silk, but what's the '9' for on your license plates?"

Reggie shifted a little as he glanced out the window. He was thinking whether he should slip into his Silk mode and really get Morris going. Instead, he turned to Morris and asked, "Do you want the real story or my 'Silk' line story?"

Morris laughed and said, "Give me the real deal."

Reggie said "okay" before beginning. "Well, the day I went to the Department of Motor Vehicles to sign up for my personalized vanity plates, I had to put down three choices on the request form. So I put down Silk, Silk 1, and Silk 2. The woman at the registration window told me that all three were already taken. Of course, I was disappointed, but I filled out another request form with Silk 3, Silk 4 and Silk 5. They were all taken too. So I thought I would change strategy and filled out another form with Roman Numerals. Silk I, Silk II, and Silk III. They were taken too. So I was really pissed. I went back to the window and asked the woman outright, 'Show me the list that should have the next available number.' She wasn't happy with my request, but when I saw the list and that Silk 9 was still on the table, I said, 'Sign me up.'"

After hearing Reggie's explanation, Morris looked at him. "That's it?"

Reggie hunched his shoulder. "Yeah, that's it."

Morris became a little more serious and said, "Sounds like you are thinking about giving up your license plates."

Reggie smiled at him and said, "Well, I wouldn't go so far as to say that, but you know."

Morris shook his head at his best friend, slapped the steering wheel, and added, "Hey, just relax and get through the rehearsal. It's not like you are going to marry one of the bridesmaids."

The word "marry" made Reggie shift his thoughts. He felt he had been remiss in not telling Morris that he was honored to be his best man.

"Hey, Morris, I know we haven't had a lot of time to really talk since I arrived, but I'm delighted that you picked me to be your best man, and more importantly, I'm really happy for you and Sheila and the fact that you found the right woman. "

Morris responded,

"Yeah, she's the one all right." As he wheeled around a corner, he looked over at his friend. "Hey, but you are still living the dream: single, successful, nice clothes, fancy car, fantastic job."

Reggie was still thinking and looked a little forlorn but said, "Yeah, but I'm still working hard with long hours. I mean, I like it because I'm the boss, but you know I haven't found one woman to really invest any quality time in. You know, someone to . . . Hey, I don't know. I guess it will happen when it happens."

Morris rolled into the parking lot a little faster than Reggie would have liked. He put the car in park, reached over, and slapped Reggie on the shoulder. "Hey, man, just keep the faith. And in the meantime, enjoy the fact that you should have at least six young ladies in there to make 'small talk' with."

They both laughed as they got out of the car.

CHAPTER 62

Sheila looked at her watch as she raced to the door to meet them. "You guys are really late, but thanks, Reggie, for getting him here. Let's go. Everyone is waiting."

They walked into the large room, and Sheila began the introductions to her parents, Morris's parents, the other groomsmen, and the minister. They walked across the room to the group of bridesmaids to begin introducing Reggie when Sheila noticed one of the maids was missing. She said to the group, "Hey, where is Mooky?"

The girls turned around, and one bridesmaid responded, "She went to the ladies' room . . . Oh, wait a minute, here she comes now."

An attractive young lady with shimmering long black hair and hoop earrings hurriedly approached the group. She stopped mid-step as she saw Reggie. Their eyes met.

"Reggie?"

Reggie just stood there in what seemed like suspended animation. He could barely move his lips. "Tracey?"

There was bewilderment from everyone, but Sheila quickly asked, "You two know each other?"

Morris turned to Sheila and asked, "She's Tracey?"

Sheila answered, "Yeah, but since our sorority days, we have called her Mooky."

Sheila hunched her shoulders. "It's a long story."

The entire back and forth and the looks of amazement on everyone faces was playing out in front of Reggie at the speed of light, but he managed to turn to Morris and asked, "You didn't know this was Tracey?"

"Hey, Reggie, I told you I don't really know any of these young ladies. I mean, I knew Sheila had college sorority sisters, and I've heard names mentioned from time to time, but, hey, I had no idea that they all went to the same college as Tracey. When I think about it, man, you never told me what college Tracey attended. You just said down South."

Morris shook his head. "Hey, I know I'm smart, but no way I would have made the connection."

Reggie turned back and looked at Tracey, who appeared to be in a trance.

"Tracey . . . I can't . . . I can't believe this."

"Neither can I, Reggie . . . Neither can I."

The group was silent as the two stared at each other, both trying to say something, but no words were being uttered.

Reggie shook his head and simply said again, "I can't believe this."

Finally, Morris chimed in and spoke for the group: "Well, none of us can believe this . . . so now what?"

With a smile from ear to ear, Reggie softly answered, "I know what." He reached out his hand to Tracey. She didn't hesitate and placed her hands in his as they took a few steps away from the group.

Morris looked at the two and said, "Okay, okay. I get it. You two have a lot of catching up to do." He patted Reggie on the shoulder and smiled. "But after the rehearsal, Mr. Best Man."

Reggie squeezed Tracey's hand a little tighter, smiled, and nodded to Morris.

The minister walked over to the group and looked at Reggie and Tracey.

"Well, now that we know who's who, we still have a wedding scheduled. So ladies and gentlemen, let's take our places."

ACKNOWLEDGEMENTS

I would like to thank the following people: My wife, Carol for her continuous support through the many years that it took me to complete my manuscript. Amy Collins a great author for her wonderful writing class that inspired me to write on and complete my manuscript. In her class, incomplete was not an option. Also, a big thanks to Tom Wray, my fellow first time author and friend who kept me focused and motivated to stay the course. Andi Cumbo-Floyd was very instrumental in the early stages of my manuscript and her editing suggestions set the tone for my manuscript. Finally, the fantastic editing team of the Bookish Fox, (Sarah, Kathryn, Linda and Hannah). All of you were professional, very helpful and made my challenging manuscript better than I could ever have imagined. Thank you all.